UGLY KICKS

UGLY KICKS
Kelsey Blair

James Lorimer & Company Ltd., Publishers
Toronto

James Lorimer & Company Ltd., Publishers acknowledges the support
of the Ontario Arts Council. We acknowledge the support of the Canada
Council for the Arts which last year invested $24.3 million in writing
and publishing throughout Canada. We acknowledge the Government of
Ontario through the Ontario Media Development Corporation's Ontario
Book Initiative.

Cover image: Shutterstock

Library and Archives Canada Cataloguing in Publication

Blair, Kelsey, author
    Ugly kicks / Kelsey Blair.

(Sports stories)
Issued in print and electronic formats.
ISBN 978-1-4594-0972-9 (paperback).--ISBN 978-1-4594-0974-3 (epub)

    I. Title. II. Series: Sports stories (Toronto, Ont.)

PS8603.L3154U44 2015   jC813'.6   C2015-903543-0
                                                        C2015-903544-9

James Lorimer & Company Ltd., Publishers 317 Adelaide Street West, Suite 1002 Toronto, ON, Canada M5V 1P9 www.lorimer.ca	Canadian edition (978-1-4594-0972-9) distributed by: Formac Lorimer Books 5502 Atlantic Street Halifax, NS, Canada B3H 1G4	American edition (978-1-4594-0973-6) distributed by: Lerner Publishing Gro 1251 Washington Ave Minneapolis, MN, US 55401

Printed and bound in Canada.
Manufactured by Friesens Corporation in Altona, Manitoba, Canada
in August 2015
Job # 215808

For the women who have taught, mentored, and coached me: Barbara Walter, Shawn White, Shannon Graham, Sue Kennedy, Kathy Mulder, Deb Huband, Kirsty Johnston, and Claire Robson.

And for my parents, always.

CONTENTS

1 THE FIRST TRYOUT

Ashley Rivera sits in the passenger seat of her middle school basketball coach's car. Her knees bounce up and down.

"Don't be nervous," Stephanie says encouragingly. "It's just like any other basketball practice."

"A tryout is nothing like a practice. People get cut at the end."

"Work your hardest. That's all any coach can ask for." Stephanie pulls into the high school parking lot where the Vancouver City Regional Team tryouts are being held. She turns to Ashley, her face serious. "I know we've talked about this, but just because I'm friends with your brother and I coached your Grade 8 team, doesn't mean —"

"I'll get any special treatment," interrupts Ashley. "I'm just glad you're the assistant coach, so at least I'll know someone."

"By the end of today, you'll know everyone."

When Ashley walks into the gym, she sees a few

girls gathered in the bleachers. Ashley sits down behind them.

"Nice shoes, Jane," says one of the girls.

"I know, right?" says Jane proudly. Her shoes are neon pink with white trim. Against the white of her socks and the milky brown of her skin, the colours really stand out. "My mom bought them for me in Seattle." She leans back to make more space for herself and accidentally bumps Ashley's knee. "Sorry."

"It's okay," says Ashley.

"I'm Jane."

"Ashley."

"What do you think?" asks Jane, wiggling her shoes so Ashley can admire them.

"They're sweet."

"Yeah, they are."

Ashley hesitates before pulling her shoes out of her backpack. She doesn't own proper basketball shoes. Instead, she uses an old pair of running shoes. The laces are slightly frayed and the soles a little worn, but the shoes fit perfectly. To keep them clean, Ashley no longer wears her "basketball shoes" outside.

On the court, several girls casually shoot at one of the gym's main hoops. At the other end of the court, one girl shoots alone. Her black hair is streaked with bright purple. Ashley can see her thick blue eyeliner and bright mascara from across the gym. Ashley looks back and forth between the hoops.

"She's a weirdo," says Jane, noticing where Ashley is looking. "Come shoot with us at this hoop."

Ashley follows Jane and takes a few shots. She finds it hard to practice with so many girls at the same basket. Two balls shot by different girls collide in mid-air and bounce away from the net.

After a moment, the head coach blows her whistle and the players gather around her. "Welcome to the first Vancouver City Regional Team tryout! I'm Catherine Russell. You can call me Coach Catherine."

"I'm Stephanie Peters." Stephanie smiles at the group. "You can call me Stephanie."

"I want everyone to introduce themselves. First and last name, please." Coach Catherine turns to Jane. She is almost a full head taller than all the other players. "I'm Jane Dhillon."

One by one, the players introduce themselves. There are two girls named Emily at the tryout. One of them is the girl with the thick mascara and purple hair.

"My name's Emily Scott-Chang," she says. "But, to make things easy, you can call me Scotty."

"Are you sure?" asks Coach Catherine.

"Oh yeah," Scotty answers with a shrug. "It's the same thing at school. Even my teachers call me Scotty."

When introductions are finished, Coach Catherine explains the first drill. "We'll start with layups. Two lines at half-court."

Jane stands at the front of the line on the right.

Ashley lines up behind her. She can feel the butterflies in her stomach flutter.

"Regular right-handed layups," announces Coach Catherine.

Jane takes four commanding dribbles toward the basket. Moving full speed, she picks up the basketball, smoothly does her layup footwork, and gracefully scores the basket. Now it's Ashley's turn. She takes a deep breath and leans her weight forward. Ashley dribbles three times and picks up the ball. She jumps off her left foot and extends her right arm toward the basket. Ashley scores the layup.

"Good work," says Coach Catherine.

Ashley smiles proudly.

"Good work," says Coach Catherine again.

Ashley looks over her shoulder. A girl named Paige has scored her layup. Scotty explodes toward the basket with quick steps and easily puts the ball on the backboard and scores.

"Nice finish!" encourages Coach Catherine.

Ashley's smile fades, as almost every player scores their layup.

After several minutes, Coach Catherine announces, "Left-handed layups."

One after the other, the players in front of Ashley miss their left-handed layups. Scotty is next. She drives toward the basket. Unlike the other players, she uses footwork for a right-handed layup, shoots with her right hand, and easily scores.

Coach Catherine blows her whistle. "To be the best basketball player you can be, you must master both your right- and left-handed layup footwork. I'd rather you miss with the correct footwork than score with the wrong footwork."

At the front of the line, Ashley gulps. She takes two tentative dribbles with her left hand. On the third bounce, she almost loses the ball, but she is determined to use the correct footwork. Ashley jumps into the air and releases the ball. It bounces off the backboard, clanks against the rim, and falls away from the hoop.

"Great effort," says Coach Catherine.

The second time Ashley is at the front of the line, she focuses intently on the rim. When she gets to the key, she jumps into the air and releases the ball, but her shot is too hard. She misses.

"Ugh!" says Ashley.

"Great footwork," Stephanie encourages. "Just soften up your shot."

Ashley only scores one left-handed layup before the first water break. As she sips her water, she feels frustration bubble inside her belly. How is she supposed to make the team if she can't score? And, if she doesn't make the team, where will she play basketball now that the school season is over? Ashley throws her water bottle on the ground.

I need to work harder in the next drill.

"Get in two lines on the baseline," instructs Coach Catherine. There are two cones at different lengths from the basket. "Balls in this line," she continues, signalling at the line farthest from the basket. "This drill is called Chase. When Stephanie says go, the players at the front of each line are going to sprint toward their cones. The person in the outside line has to dribble around the cone and then come back and do a layup. The person in this line," says Coach Catherine, signalling at the line closest to the basket, "has to run outside their cone and try and challenge the dribbler's layup."

At the front of the line, Jane stands with a ball in her hand. A girl called Maude stands in the opposite line.

"Go!" yells Stephanie.

Maude chases Jane and jumps to challenge the layup, but Jane scores easily.

"I'll catch you next time," says Maude.

"Doubt it," Jane replies with a huge grin.

When Ashley gets to the front of the defensive line, she waits for Stephanie's signal.

"Go!"

Ashley pushes off her back foot and strides forward. She beats her opponent to the cone and quickly pivots. When the offensive player rounds her cone, she's surprised to see Ashley in front of her. The player bounces the ball off Ashley's foot.

"Nice defence," Jane calls from the baseline.

"Yeah," adds Maude, following Jane's cue. "Good work!"

Ashley goes to the baseline. When she gets to the front of the line, she's matched up against Jane. Jane holds the ball close to her hip. Ashley rocks her weight to the balls of her feet.

"Go!" yells Stephanie.

Ashley strides forward. Jane's long legs propel her, and the two girls reach the cone at the same time. Ashley turns. Smaller and faster than Jane, she gains a half-step. Unused to being challenged, Jane doesn't bother to protect the ball. Ashley reaches out and easily swats the ball away. Jane stops dead in her tracks with a shocked expression on her face.

"Well done!" encourages Coach Catherine.

Ashley smiles as she returns to the baseline.

After the tryout ends, the players gather around Coach Catherine. "Stephanie will give you an information sheet for your parents. This includes information about the regional team schedule. I know many of you play other sports. If you have any conflicts, I want you to let me know at the start of the next tryout."

Stephanie hands Ashley a piece of paper. Ashley casually skims the information. When she gets to the bottom, her heart jumps into her throat.

The team participation fee two hundred dollars.

2 DECISIONS

Ashley sits at her desk and stares at a math worksheet.

If two trains leave the station at the same time . . . *will Mom be able to afford the regional team fee? If she can't afford the participation fee, should I still attend the second tryout?*

Ashley shakes her head and tries to get rid of the distracting thoughts. She stares at the question. If two trains leave the station . . .

The lunch bell rings. Ashley shoves the unfinished worksheet into her bag and stands up.

At the desk beside her, her friend Tanya gets to her feet as well. "Did you watch the music video count-down last night?" she asks. Ashley nods. "Wasn't the Wade video awesome?"

"It was . . . okay."

"Okay?" asks Tanya, her dark eyes wide.

"It was just Wade, wandering down a beach."

"With his guitar," adds Tamara, Tanya's twin sis-ter, startling Ashley. She's still thinking about that registration fee. "Don't forget his guitar."

"Hurry up," says Tanya, her dark hair bouncing as she tries to move Ashley along.

"Why?"

"The track team meeting is at lunch today. You should come join!" When she sees Ashley hesitate, she says, "Tamara's joining too."

"Of course she is."

"Just because we're twins doesn't mean we do everything together," protests Tamara.

"Tell me something you don't do together," challenges Ashley.

Tamara crinkles her brow. "I'll come up with something. Come on."

"Yeah, and . . ." Ashley hesitates. She doesn't want to disappoint the twins. "I don't think I'm doing track this year."

"What?" ask Tanya and Tamara in unison.

"I want to focus on basketball." She pauses. "If I make the team," she adds quietly.

There's a moment of silence. Ashley holds her breath.

"It'll suck not seeing you," says Tanya. "But, you can always meet up with us after practice!"

"Totally," says Ashley, breathing a sigh of relief.

"And you'll make the team."

"I hope so."

Ugly Kicks

★★★

"Mom!" Ashley yells as she opens the front door of their apartment.

"Ashley!" Ashley's mom mimics her shout. She comes out of the kitchen with her arms open wide and pulls Ashley into a big hug.

"You smell like French fries," says Ashley, pulling away.

"I just got home from Something Fishy."

"But today's Tuesday. Don't you usually work at the shoe store on Tuesdays?"

"I've taken a few extra shifts at the restaurant, so I'll be doing double duty on Mondays, Tuesdays, and Saturdays."

Ashley hesitates. "I need to talk to you about something."

"Come into the kitchen and tell me."

"The regional team coach gave us an information sheet last night," Ashley says as her mom sits down. Still standing, Ashley hands her mom the sheet and watches her read. Her expression is very serious. She motions for Ashley to join her at the table.

"It costs two hundred dollars." Her mom sighs. Ashley hates it when her mom gets upset. Ashley knows what she has to do. It's the same thing she did when her mom couldn't afford to send Ashley to band camp with Tanya and Tamara over spring break.

Ashley takes a deep breath. "I won't go to the second tryout."

There's a long silence. Ashley's mom looks away. Her gaze is distant, as though she's staring at the ocean. When she finally looks back at Ashley, she says, "I think you should go. Attending tryouts is a good experience."

"But what if I make the team?"

"We'll cross that bridge when we get there."

A smile creeps onto Ashley's lips. She really loves playing basketball.

"I can't make any promises," her mom warns her.

"I know," replies Ashley.

"Okay. Now go tell Stephanie and Matt that I brought home dinner from the restaurant."

"Stephanie's here? Cool."

Ashley walks down the hallway to where her brother Matt's door is ajar. She pushes it open. She sees Stephanie sitting at Matt's desk, studying. Matt is lying on his bed, staring at the ceiling.

"Hey, Ash!" Stephanie says warmly.

Matt looks in Ashley's direction but doesn't say anything. His brown hair looks like it hasn't been brushed in days.

"Mom wants me to tell you that dinner's ready. It's from the restaurant."

"Sounds great," says Stephanie, closing her textbook and getting up.

"Meh," says Matt. He makes no effort to move.

"Since when don't you like food?" teases Stephanie. Ashley has no idea why someone as cool as Stephanie would be friends with her brother. Stephanie turns to Ashley. "What did you think of the tryout last night?"

"It was all right, I guess. I missed a lot of the left-handed layups."

"But you used the proper footwork. That's important."

Matt finally stands and looks at Stephanie. "I can't believe you're coaching the regional team. You just finished coaching Ash's school team."

"Once I'm done, I'll have completed all my volunteer hours," says Stephanie proudly.

"Overachiever," mutters Matt.

"Better than being an underachiever," replies Stephanie, sticking out her tongue. "Besides, I really like coaching. I'm starving. Let's eat."

3 MAKING THE TEAM

Ashley stands at centre court while Coach Catherine announces partners for a shooting game. She shakes her hand to try and get rid of the nervous feeling tingling in her palms. At the end of this tryout, the team will be selected.

"Paige and Brea, you'll be partners," Coach Catherine says. Paige gives Brea a high-five. This leaves Jane, Scotty, Ashley, and Leanne. Ashley hopes that she's paired with Jane so that they can win the drill and Ashley can make a good impression on the coach. "Leanne and Jane, you'll be partners."

"Sweet," says Leanne.

"It'll only be sweet if we win," says Jane. "You better do your part." Leanne's eyes go wide but Jane just laughs.

Ashley sighs and walks to join Scotty.

"Could you at least pretend not to be disappointed you're paired with me?" snarls Scotty.

"I'm not disappointed I'm paired with you," Ashley fires back. This is true. She's disappointed she *wasn't* paired with Jane, but she doesn't mind being paired with Scotty.

"You sure about that?"

"Well, I'm less sure now," grumbles Ashley, frustrated with Scotty's attitude.

To Ashley's surprise, Scotty doesn't get angry. Instead, a small smile crosses her face.

Coach Catherine clears her throat. "Players will alternate taking shots. You get one point for a scored basket inside the key, two points for a basket outside the key, and three points for a three-point shot. Keep track of your team's score out loud. First up, Brea's team versus Ashley's."

"Wanna be the first shooter?" asks Scotty.

"Sure." Ashley takes the ball. She looks down the other end of the court. Brea walks outside the three-point line and signals for her partner to pass her the ball. Ashley moves to stand outside her own three-point line.

Stephanie blows the whistle. Ashley shoots a three-point shot and misses. At the other end of the court, Ashley hears Brea's team yell out, "Three!"

Ashley passes the ball to Scotty. She shoots and scores.

"Two!" yells Ashley. She looks to the other end where Brea lines up and takes another three-point shot. Not wanting to fall behind by three more points, Ashley shoots a three. She misses and is forced to chase after another long rebound. She passes the ball to Scotty.

"Four!" yells Ashley, as Scotty scores.

At the other end of the court, Brea is lining up outside the three-point line again. Ashley hesitates.

"Take a one-pointer," instructs Scotty. Ashley does as she's told. She scores. "Five!" Scotty shouts.

At the other end, Brea yells out, "Six!"

Ashley passes the ball to Scotty. She shoots and misses, but the rebound falls directly in Ashley's hands. Without thinking, she shoots and scores.

"Six," yells Ashley. She passes the ball to Scotty, who scores two points. "Eight!"

"Twenty seconds left," yells Stephanie. Ashley and Scotty get into a groove; Ashley shoots one-point shots and Scotty shoots two-point shots. "Five seconds!"

"Twenty," yell the girls at the other end.

Ashley scores a one-point basket. "Nineteen." She passes the ball to Scotty.

"Three, two . . ." yells Stephanie. Scotty releases the ball. It hits the backboard and swishes through the hoop. "One! Time's up!"

"Twenty-one," say Scotty and Ashley in unison.

"Ashley's team wins," says Coach Catherine. "Next up, Jane's team will play Lucy's team."

Ashley and Scotty stand on the sideline and watch the other teams.

"Nice shot at the end," says Ashley to Scotty.

Scotty nods, but her stare is focused intently on the court.

Stephanie blows the whistle. Jane shoots and scores a three-point shot.

"Three!" yells Leanne.

Scotty blinks several times as she watches the players on the court shoot. Her thick mascara accentuates every eyelid movement. Scotty turns to Ashley. "Do you shoot threes in games?"

"Never."

"Me neither. We're not shooting threes."

"Twenty-five!" says Jane, as she scores another three-point shot.

"We'll never win if we're only going by ones and twos," argues Ashley.

"That time when you got your own rebound and passed it to me . . . that was good. It was fast. What if you only shoot one-pointers and I only shoot two-pointers, but you get all the rebounds?" On the court, Jane's team easily beats their opponent. Another competition begins. "If we can get more shots up than the other teams, it should make up for not shooting threes."

Ashley wants to win. "Sure. Let's try it."

After a few more matchups, the second round begins.

"Ashley's team versus Jocelyn's team," announces Coach Catherine.

Ashley and Scotty go to the hoop. Scotty passes Ashley the ball. "You start. Get us an easy point."

Ashley nods. Stephanie blows the whistle. Ashley shoots and scores.

"One," says Scotty.

Ashley immediately grabs the rebound and passes it to Scotty who shoots and scores.

"Three," they both say at once. Scotty was right. With Ashley rebounding, Scotty and Ashley are able to get up more shots than the other team. When Stephanie blows the whistle to signal the end of the game, Ashley and Scotty beat Jocelyn's team by seven points.

At the end of the round, Coach Catherine announces, "We've got two teams left: Scotty and Ashley, and Jane and Leanne. After a quick water break, they'll square off!"

While Ashley goes to the bleachers to get her water, she thinks about squaring off against Jane. Ashley's not sure what it is, but there's something about Jane that gets her noticed. Maybe it's because she's one of the best players in the gym. Maybe it's her gorgeous shoes and matching shorts. Whatever it is, Ashley wants Jane to like her, and judging from the girls gathered around Jane, so do they.

"Nice shooting," says Jane to Ashley, her tone a little teasing.

"You too," replies Ashley. "You ready for the final?"

"Of course. Are you ready?"

As Ashley bends over to pick up her water bottle, Jane leans in slightly. With a mocking tone, she says, "I hope you shoot lots of threes."

Is Jane making fun of her three-point shootings?

Ashley stands up to her full height. "What does that mean?" Her tone is sharper than she'd planned. Jane steps closer until they're nose to nose.

"Whoa," says Scotty, grabbing Ashley's wrist and tugging her down the bleacher steps.

"Did she just make fun of my shooting?"

"Probably," says Scotty. "You should take it as a compliment."

"How is *that* a compliment?"

"If she didn't think you could beat her, she wouldn't say anything."

"We've got to win," Ashley growls. "Maybe we should take some threes?"

"Absolutely not. We've got to stick to the plan. When you get a rebound, I'm going to move to the opposite side, so that when you score, I'll be right in front of you."

Ashley nods and goes to her spot. At the other end of the court, Jane lines up at the three-point line. Stephanie blows the whistle.

Ashley shoots and scores. "One!"

As the ball falls through the mesh, Jane hollers, "Three!" More focused on Jane than on her own basket, Ashley fumbles the rebound.

"Ignore them," instructs Scotty. Ashley passes her the ball. She shoots.

"Three," says Ashley as the ball goes through the net. At the other end of the court, Ashley hears "Six!"

She looks down the court to see Jane with a wide smile on her face.

"Ignore them!" says Scotty, more harshly this time.

Ashley shoots and scores. She immediately grabs her own rebound and looks up. Just as she'd promised, Scotty is standing right in front of her. Ashley passes her the ball and backs up to get ready for the next rebound. Ashley gets into a rhythm: shoot, rebound, pass; shoot, rebound, pass. As she concentrates, she stops hearing Jane on the other end of the court.

"Three seconds," calls Stephanie. "Two . . ."

Scotty shoots the ball and scores. In her rhythm, Ashley gets the rebound and releases another quick shot.

". . . One!"

The ball goes through the hoop.

"Thirty-two," yells Scotty as Stephanie blows the whistle.

Ashley looks around. She has no idea how many points Jane and Leanne have.

"Thirty-two to thirty-one," says Coach Catherine. "Good job, Ashley and Scotty!"

"No way," says Jane aloud.

"Jane," says Coach Catherine curtly, "Is there something you'd like to say?"

"No," Jane says quickly. She shoots a glare at Leanne and crosses her arms over her chest.

Scotty walks over to Ashley and holds out her hand

for a high-five. Suddenly, Ashley feels the eyes of all the other players watching them. Ashley looks at Scotty's dark makeup and purple hair. She limply slaps Scotty's palm.

"Weakest high-five ever." Scotty raises an eyebrow, as though she knows exactly what Ashley is thinking.

Before Ashley can say anything, Scotty jogs to the bleachers to grab her water bottle.

After a water break, the tryout continues. Energized from the win, Ashley works hard, but with every minute, her nerves grow. When Coach Catherine blows the whistle to signal the end of the tryout, Ashley's heart is pounding.

The players gather at centre court. "It's been a great two days of tryouts," begins Coach Catherine. "I'm going to read off a list of names. If you hear your name, you have been selected for the team. Jane Dhillon, Paige Smith, Maude Randall, Emily Scott-Chang." Ashley's heart thumps in her chest. "Ashley Rivera."

Ashley doesn't hear any of the other names on the list. She made the team!

"Congratulations to those of you who made the team. Please bring the registration form and fee by the end of next week. Scotty, can you please come and talk to me for a moment?"

All of the excitement drains from Ashley's body. What if her mom can't pay the fee? Will she have to quit the team?

Suddenly, an arm wraps around Ashley's shoulder. "Looks like we're going to be teammates," says Jane. Before Ashley can respond, Jane leans toward her ear. "No hard feelings about earlier, yeah? I was just messing around."

"It's okay," says Ashley, distracted.

"Awesome." Jane squeezes Ashley's shoulder before walking to the bleachers and greeting several of her new teammates with high-fives. Ashley wants nothing more than to be one of their teammates too.

4 MONEY, MONEY, MONEY

Ashley sits in the corner of her living room, curled up on a small blue chair. Matt lies on the couch, stretched out like a sloth. He is still wearing his work uniform from his after-school job. Their mom sits beside him, squeezed between his feet at the couch's armrest. She holds the regional team information sheet in her hand. She looks at Ashley.

"Things have been slow at Something Fishy this month," begins her mom. "We could do fifty dollars or even seventy-five, but two hundred . . . I'm so sorry, Ashley, but we just can't afford it."

Ashley bites her bottom lip to stop it from shaking. She knows that crying will make her mom even more upset. "I understand."

"I wish you didn't have to understand," says her mom. She gets up and kisses Ashley on the forehead. "But I have to get to work. I'll be home late tonight. Matt, make sure Ashley gets to bed on time."

"I can get myself to bed," Ashley says.

"I know you can, but it's good for your brother to have something to do," her mom says with a wink. As she goes to the door, the buzzer rings. "Hello? Come on in, Stephanie."

When Ashley's mom is about to leave, Stephanie crosses paths with her at the door. "Hi, Mrs. Rivera."

"Hello, Stephanie. Matt, get up and say hello to your friend."

"Steph doesn't need me to get up for her," yawns Matt.

"But I bet she'd like it."

Matt doesn't move. Ashley's mom sighs and leaves.

With her mom gone, Ashley doesn't have to be strong anymore. The tears welling in her eyes drip down her cheeks.

"Ashley! What's the matter?" Stephanie asks, her voice full of concern.

"She can't play on the regional team. We can't afford the fee," says Matt bluntly.

"Oh," says Stephanie. "I'm really sorry to hear that." There's a moment of silence. "But, maybe there are other options."

"There are no other options," Matt grumbles. Last year, Tanya thought Matt was the second-cutest boy on the planet (just after Wade, of course). Now, Matt's work uniform is baggy, and his hair is greasy. Ashley wonders what Tanya thinks of him this year. "She should just quit the team."

"No, she shouldn't," says Stephanie firmly. "Not without exhausting our options."

"Our?"

"What is up with you?" snaps Stephanie. "Playing on the regional team is a great opportunity for Ashley. She'll get to practice with the best players in Vancouver and play against the best players in the province. And Catherine's great."

"Is Catherine so great that she'll waive the fee?" Matt asks sarcastically. Stephanie clenches her jaw, but doesn't answer. "I didn't think so."

"There might be other ways."

"Doubt it."

"Ashley could apply for funding."

"The fee is due next week," Ashley murmurs from her corner.

Stephanie starts pacing back and forth. "What about a bake sale? She could come to the high school and sell cupcakes. Who doesn't like cupcakes?"

"She's going to sell two hundred dollars' worth of cupcakes?" Matt rolls his eyes.

"It's not impossible."

"We can't afford it," argues Matt. Stephanie starts pacing faster. "Why do you care so much anyways?"

Stephanie stops and turns in one motion. She looks at Matt with an expression so fierce, Ashley's surprised he doesn't melt under her glare. "Because I'm her school coach, and I care about my players. Because even if there are things Ashley can't do because of her situation, there might be other things she can do, and she won't know without trying. Because she's *your* younger sister!" Stephanie takes a deep breath. "I think the better question is why don't *you* care?"

Matt crosses his arms over his chest and looks at the ceiling. "Whatever."

Stephanie scoffs and begins pacing again. There's a long silence.

Ashley assumed that if her mom didn't have the money, she wouldn't be able to play on the regional team, but what if that wasn't true? Maybe she needs to look at things differently. "I have some money from babysitting for Mrs. Greene," offers Ashley. "I was saving it up for the Wade concert in the summer."

"Well, would you rather spend it on basketball or on the Wade concert?" asks Stephanie.

"Basketball," Ashley answers instantly. "I've got about twenty-five dollars saved."

"That's a start."

"And mom said she might be able to afford seventy-five."

"Good," says Stephanie. "So, you need one hundred more."

"I wish the fee wasn't due this week," says Ashley. "Then I'd have more time to save my babysitting money."

Stephanie stops pacing. "That's it!"

"What's it?"

"Maybe Catherine can ask the league to let you pay the fee in installments. Do you want me to talk to her?"

"That'd be great," says Ashley.

"Good," says Matt. "Now, can we stop hanging out with my baby sister?"

"Hey!"

"What's up with you?" asks Stephanie.

"Nothing," grumbles Matt. His arms are still crossed tightly across his chest.

"It's okay," says Ashley. "I'll go."

As Ashley heads for her room, she overhears Matt and Stephanie in the living room.

"Seriously, Matt," says Stephanie. "You were so mean to Ashley. What's wrong?"

"This is a bad idea," Matt sighs. "She's just going to be disappointed."

"Why are you being so negative?"

"I'm just trying to protect her. Look at me. Last year, I was the star of the soccer team. I was going to get a scholarship from a big university. Then, bam! I injured my knee. I can't afford to go to university without a scholarship. I can't play soccer . . ." Matt hesitates. "Which isn't the end of the world." His voice quivers. "I don't even really like it."

"Liar. You love soccer."

"Not anymore," snaps Matt. "I had to work two jobs to afford physiotherapy. It sucked. And, now that

I'm not the star of any team, no one cares about me anymore."

"How can you think that?" asks Stephanie. Ashley can't see Stephanie's face, but her voice sounds both worried and hurt.

"How can I not?"

Ashley gets to her room and Stephanie and Matt's voices fade, leaving her alone with her thoughts.

Why does playing basketball have to cost so much? What if Coach Catherine says no?

5 WHAT IT'S WORTH

Beep! Beep! Beep!

Ashley rolls over and looks over at her alarm clock. The bright red numbers read 7:15 a.m.

"Ugh," Ashley groans as she rolls out of bed.

When she walks into the kitchen, her mom greets her. "Morning! You're up early."

"I'm getting a ride to school with Tanya and Tamara," says Ashley. "They've got track practice."

Ashley's mom looks past her shoulder and frowns. "Where's your brother?"

"In bed?"

Ashley's mom throws down the dishtowel she's holding. "

What's wrong, Mom?"

"He's supposed to be at physiotherapy for his knee."

"He is?"

"I just arranged it with the local clinic. They said if he comes in before business hours, he can have physiotherapy for a reduced price. He was working so hard at

36

getting his knee better. I don't understand what happened." Her mom sighs and holds up a piece of paper with a phone number written on it. "And I wanted to give to him this."

"What is it?"

"A friend of mine is looking for someone to deliver newspapers. I said Matt might be interested."

"Could I do it?"

"This has to do with the basketball team, doesn't it?"

"Yeah," admits Ashley. "Stephanie said she'd talk to Coach Catherine for me."

"I know."

"You do?"

"Catherine called this morning. She talked to the league, and they're willing to extend the fee deadline so we can pay in installments."

"I can play?!" Ashley's heart leaps into her throat. "Really?!"

"We can't afford the extra money right now."

"But that's why the paper route would be perfect!" argues Ashley. "Between that and babysitting, I'll be able to save enough to pay the fee!"

"That's a lot to take on."

"For basketball, it'll be worth it."

"Are you sure you want to play basketball that badly?"

"Yes, Mom, I'm sure."

"Okay. Let's give it a try, but if it's too much, I want

you to tell me." Ashley nods and her mom gives her the piece of paper. "Give Mr. Penumbra a call."

"Thanks!"

Her mom marches down the hall to wake Matt. Ashley grabs her backpack and speed-walks out the apartment door. Just as she opens the lobby entrance, the twins' car rolls up; their dad is at the wheel. Ashley hustles down the sidewalk and hops in the back seat.

"Morning!" Tanya and Tamara say brightly.

"Morning," replies Ashley.

"The girls told me you made the regional basketball team," Tamara and Tanya's dad says. "How are you enjoying it?"

"I really like it so far," replies Ashley. "We've got practice tonight."

"But the new countdown premieres tonight," whines Tanya. "You missed the last one too."

Tanya looks genuinely upset that Ashley can't watch the countdown.

"Maybe I can try and come after basketball?" offers Ashley.

Tanya's face lights up. "That'd be awesome."

When they reach the school, Tanya, Tamara, and Ashley pile out of the car and walk toward the field. Tanya and Tamara join the crowd gathered around Mr. Jones, the track team coach. Ashley walks away from the field and toward the school. She takes out Matt's old cell phone and presses the "on" button.

"Come on," grumbles Ashley.

I wish I had a brand-new phone.

She carefully presses the button again. The phone buzzes. Ashley pulls out the piece of paper with the phone number scribbled on it and dials.

"Hello," says a stern male voice.

"Hello," Ashley says nervously. "My mom told me to call you about a paper route."

"And who is your mom?"

"Lenora Rivera," answers Ashley.

"Oh!" His voice is suddenly much brighter. "Tell me a bit about yourself."

"My name is Ashley. I babysit for my neighbour, and I'm very responsible."

"Well, if your mom sent you, it must be true! I need someone to deliver newspapers three days a week. Mondays, Thursdays, and Saturdays. Paper pickup time is 5:30 a.m. on weekdays and 7:30 a.m. on weekends. Think you can do that?"

Ashley imagines herself wearing the regional team jersey. "I do."

"Can you start this week?"

"I can."

"Then you're hired."

Ashley hangs up the phone and squeals with delight. She gets to play basketball!

★★★

Ashley stands at Mrs. Greene's door, putting on her shoes.

"*Moooom*! Jeremy stole my teapot!" shouts Mrs. Greene's daughter, Sarah.

"Did not!" argues Sarah's younger brother, Jeremy.

"No arguing," says Mrs. Greene. "Did you have a good time with Ashley today?"

"Yes!" They both squeal in unison.

"She helped me with my picture!" says Jeremy.

"And we had tea!" adds Sarah.

"Imaginary tea," explains Ashley. "We ate apple slices with peanut butter for an after-school snack."

"Sounds like a busy afternoon," says Mrs. Greene. She hands Ashley money for the afternoon's work. Ashley puts the bills into a white envelope marked "installment" that she's going to give to Stephanie at practice. "Ashley, before you go . . . I know you usually only babysit on Tuesdays, but things are crazy at work this month. Do you think you could do another day?"

More babysitting means more money for the participation fee. "That'd be great, actually. Thanks, Mrs. Greene."

"Good. Can you start this Thursday?"

"Sure."

6 NICE KICKS

Ashley rushes out of the apartment and busses to practice. When she gets to the gym, she jogs to fill her water bottle. She swings open the washroom door and sees Scotty sitting on a bench with a cloth in her hand. She sniffles and looks up at Ashley. There are tears in her eyes.

"You okay?" asks Ashley.

"Do I look okay?" snaps Scotty. She wipes makeup from her cheeks.

Ashley decides to ignore Scotty's sharp tone. "What are you doing?"

"The Provincial Tournament has rules about makeup."

"Really?"

"I can't wear anything that might rub off because other players could be allergic." Scotty's bottom lip trembles as she wipes eye shadow from her eyes. "Which is stupid. My makeup would never rub off." Scotty sighs. "Coach Catherine says I should probably practice without my makeup, so I can get used to it."

Scotty looks at herself in the mirror. No furrowed eyebrows. No harsh glare. Just wide eyes filled with tears.

Ashley hears footsteps outside the washroom door.

"Scotty! Where are you?" shouts Jane from outside the door.

Scotty leaps up and runs into a washroom stall. She closes the stall door just as the washroom door opens.

Jane stands at the doorway, her eyebrow raised as she surveys the room. "Have you seen Scotty?"

"No." Ashley answers before she even thinks about it.

Jane rolls her eyes. "Ugh! I can't find my water bottle. I bet I put it in her bag on the way here. Whatever, Maude will share." Jane leaves. Ashley hears her footsteps stomp down the hallway.

Scotty unlatches the washroom door.

"What was that about?" asks Ashley.

"I don't need her seeing me cry," replies Scotty. "Why'd you lie for me?"

"I dunno," says Ashley, shrugging. "I just did."

Scotty stares at Ashley as though she's a puzzle. "Maybe you're all right."

"Maybe?"

"Take it or leave it."

"Can I ask you something?"

"You just did."

Ashley rolls her eyes. "Why would you have Jane's water bottle?"

Nice Kicks

"We're neighbours. Our parents make us carpool together."

"So you go to the same school?"

"Unfortunately." Scotty puts her makeup cloth away. "My mom told her mom about not being able to wear makeup for basketball. She was teasing me about it in the car."

"So, that's why you're crying . . ." A blush fills Scotty's cheeks and she looks to the ground. "I mean . . . that sucks."

"It does, but whatever. You need to leave."

"What? Why?"

"If we walk out together, Jane will know you were lying."

"Oh. Right."

Most of the team's players are already gathering. Ashley quickly changes her shoes and jogs onto the court. Moments later, Scotty follows.

"You're not wearing any mascara," blurts out Jocelyn suddenly. Several players turn to look at Scotty. "Or any eyeliner. Or any eye shadow. Or any blush." Jocelyn squints her eyes to examine Scotty more closely. "You're not wearing lipstick either. "

"Thanks for pointing that out," replies Scotty sharply.

Jane opens her mouth to speak, but Coach Catherine blows her whistle to signal the beginning of practice. "This year, to make games at the tournament fairly

43

matched, the Provincial Tournament organizers have divided the tournament into Tier One and Tier Two. The Tier Two tournament will be held in Burnaby."

"My mom works in Burnaby," says Jocelyn. "She takes the bus."

"If we make the Tier Two Tournament, she can help us organize how to get there," replies Coach Catherine. "But, our goal is to make the Tier One Tournament, which will be held in Victoria."

A murmur of excitement runs through the team.

Victoria is a two-hour ferry ride away.

Ashley's heart thumps painfully.

Ferry rides cost money.

"Does that mean that we're going on an away trip?" asks Maude.

"Possibly," replies Coach Catherine. "Obviously, if we go to Victoria, there will be additional costs."

Ashley squeezes her eyes shut. *Another fee?*

"So, how do we make the Tier One Tournament?" asks Jane.

"In addition to our tournaments and exhibition games, we're in a round robin playoff pool with three other regional teams, Burnaby, New Westminster, and Richmond. Over the next few weeks, we'll play one game against each team. The top two teams from each pool will go to the Tier One Tournament."

"Fun," says Paige.

"Winning games starts in practice," begins Coach

Catherine. "We're going to start today's practice with the Chase drill . . . on the left side of the court. Anyone who doesn't shoot with their left hand will have to do ten push-ups."

"Great," murmurs Scotty.

The players line up on the baseline. Ashley feels a twinkle of excitement her chest. She's never played in a top-tier provincial tournament before! Suddenly, the energy she used for babysitting causes Ashley's mouth to open into a wide yawn. Then, a feeling of dread fills her body.

How can I afford to go to Victoria?

Ashley's muscles tighten. She shakes her arms to get rid of the feeling and focuses her attention on the drill. Scotty and Jane are paired up against each other, with Jane on defence.

"Go!" yells Stephanie. Jane and Scotty immediately sprint toward the cone. Scotty gets to her cone first and turns the corner, but Jane isn't far behind. Scotty jumps into the air to complete her layup, but she uses her left hand. Her shot clanks against the front of the rim.

"Nice try!" encourages Stephanie from the sideline. "Keep practicing with your left hand."

"Yeah . . . nice try." Jane smirks.

Scotty glares at her.

When Ashley reaches the front of the defensive line, she's paired against Maude.

"Go!"

Ashley's legs feel heavy. When she reaches the cone, she immediately turns in the other direction. Maude is a half-step in front of Ashley, forcing Ashley to chase her from behind. Ashley tries to accelerate but her legs won't move any faster. Maude scores her left-handed layup.

"Good work, Maude!" calls Stephanie.

Frustrated with herself, Ashley moves to the back of the line.

A few turns later, Scotty is at the front of the offensive line, still matched up against Jane.

"Go!" yells Stephanie.

Scotty pushes the ball out farther in front of her to capitalize on her speed. Eager to block Scotty's shot, Jane leaps into the air. But, instead of finishing on the left-hand side of the basket, Scotty reaches underneath the basket and scores with her right hand.

"Whoa," says Maude on the baseline. "Nice finish."

"It was a very nice layup," says Stephanie, "but it was still with your right hand. Ten push-ups."

"Sorry," says Scotty.

"Don't be sorry." Stephanie smiles. "But don't be scared to make mistakes either. Practice is the time to try things."

Scotty nods and drops to the ground to do her push-ups.

When Ashley gets to the front of the defensive line, she's matched up against Jane.

"Go!"

Ashley sprints. Jane's strides are long, but Ashley pumps her arms and keeps her eyes locked on the cone in front of her. When she gets to the cone, she plants her foot and turns immediately. She's nose to nose with Jane. Ashley and Jane each take two steps toward the basket. Just like in the tryouts, Jane doesn't protect the ball and Ashley is able to easily swat it away.

"You've got to protect the ball," says Coach Catherine to a scowling Jane.

Maude points at Ashley's foot. "Your shoelace is undone."

Ashley bends to tie it.

"Nice kicks," Jane mutters as she passes Ashley to go to the opposite line. "Those are the ugliest basketball shoes I've ever seen."

Ashley used to like browsing for shoes with the twins. When they were younger, they couldn't buy shoes without their parents' permission, and they'd wander shoe aisles of the shoe store where Ashley's mom is still working, looking at all the most recent styles. Then the twins started getting an allowance. Now they use their savings to buy shoes. Ashley doesn't get an allowance. Sometimes she imagines the kinds of shoes she would buy if she did. They'd definitely have a high top with brightly coloured trim and neon-green shoelaces.

Ashley is at the front of the offensive line. As the group in front of them races toward the cone, Jane looks at Ashley from the front of the defensive line,

"Ready to get blocked, Sneakers?"

"Go!"

"What did you just call me?" asks Ashley, but Jane is already two full steps ahead. Ashley pushes the ball out in front of her. Rushed, she struggles to control the ball as she pounds forward. When she pivots around the cone, Jane is waiting for her. When Ashley shoots, Jane easily swats the ball away.

Jane sneers at Ashley and walks away. Ashley's stomach tightens into a knot. She clenches her fists.

Did she call me "Sneakers"?

Ashley looks down at her shoes. They really are raggedy. Ashley's cheeks fill with the heat of a blush.

Maybe she won't want to be friends with me anymore.

She looks over at Jane, laughing easily with Paige. Ashley gets in line to continue the drill, always keeping an eye on where Jane is on the court.

After practice, the players gather in the stands to remove their shoes.

"If we're going to be a team, we need to get to know each other better," announces Jane. "Let's all go for ice cream after practice!"

"I have to ask my parents," says Paige.

"Me too," says Maude.

"So ask them," replies Jane, like it's the most obvious thing in the world. Several of the girls bound up the gym stairs to talk to their parents, but Ashley doesn't move. "You're coming, right, Ash?"

The moment Jane calls her "Ash," Ashley forgets about Jane calling her "Sneakers."

"I'm supposed to get a ride home with Stephanie," Ashley answers.

"My mom will give you a ride," says Jane. "I'll go tell her."

Jane walks up to the top of the bleachers and talks to a tall lady with brown hair. The lady nods.

"Come on, Ash!" Jane calls.

On hearing "Ash" for the second time, Ashley's face flushes with excitement.

The front pocket of Ashley's backpack buzzes. Ashley opens the zipper and takes out her cell phone.

There's a text message from Tanya: "Come watch the countdown with us!!!"

Ashley moves her thumb so that it hovers over top of the keypad, but she doesn't type.

What do I say?

"You coming or what?" asks Jane from the top of the bleachers. Around Jane, the other players laugh and chat with one another.

Ashley types hurriedly: "Can't tonight. Basketball stuff!"

Tanya instantly replies with a sad face emoticon. Ashley feels a twinge of guilt, but she shakes it off and walks up the stairs to meet Jane and the rest of the team.

7 GETTING IN THE GAME

Ashley sits at a tiny table drinking imaginary tea from a miniature cup. Across from her, Sarah holds a toy teapot.

"More tea, Madame?" asks Sarah in her best English accent.

"Sure," says Ashley, with a yawn.

"Why are you yawning?" asks Sarah, annoyed.

"I had my paper route this morning."

"What's a paper route?" asks Jeremy.

"It's when you deliver newspapers to people's houses." Ashley looks up at the clock. Mrs. Greene is five minutes late. The team's first game starts in an hour.

"We're having tea, Jeremy," chides Sarah.

"Tea is stupid!" shouts Jeremy.

"Jeremy —" Ashley begins.

"No, it's not!" snaps Sarah.

"Sarah —" Ashley tries again.

"Yes it is!"

"Not!"

"Is!"

"Stop it!" says Ashley firmly.

They look at Ashley and immediately start to pout. Luckily, Ashley hears a key in the front door.

"Sorry I'm late," says Mrs. Greene as she walks into the apartment.

"No problem," Ashley lies. She scurries to pick up her backpack and put on her shoes. She shouts a farewell to the kids and rushes out the door. The bus comes at exactly 5:10 p.m. If Ashley misses it, she'll be late for the game. She looks down the street. The bus is already approaching the stop. Ashley picks up her pace and begins to run toward the road. The bus rolls to a stop just as Ashley arrives.

"Good timing!" says the jolly bus driver.

Ashley's puffs short, winded breaths from sprinting. As she sits, her stomach growls loudly. She remembered to pack a full lunch, but forgot to pack a snack for between babysitting and the game. Traffic is slow in downtown Vancouver, and Ashley bounces her knee up and down impatiently. When the bus finally reaches her stop, Ashley springs up and runs from the road to the high school's front door.

She jogs into the gym just in time to put on her uniform and join the other players for warmup. After warmup, the team gathers to listen to Coach Catherine. She draws on her coach's board. "Does everyone remember the 1–4 play we introduced last practice?" The players tentatively nod. "Scotty, as the point guard, where do you go in 1–4?"

"I dribble at the top while everyone else runs to their positions."

"Right," says Coach Catherine, drawing Scotty's explanation. "Jane, where does everyone else go in 1–4?"

"We go to the baseline. One player on each side of the key, one player in each corner."

"Good. When everyone's set, the point guard makes a move to beat her defender." She looks at Scotty. "If another defender steps in to stop you, you pass. Otherwise, you look to score." She looks at the rest of the players. "If the point guard drives in your direction, you have to move to get open. Got it?" The team nods. "Scotty, Leanne, Jocelyn, Paige, and Jane, you're going to start. Let's work hard out there, ladies. 'Vancouver' on three. One. Two. Three . . ."

"Vancouver!"

Ashley takes a spot on the bench. On court, the starting players for each team line up around the tip-off circle. Jane stands at the centre for the tip-off. Ashley notices that Jane, who looks so tall in practice, isn't any taller than her defender, wearing Burnaby royal purple.

"That's Kelly Pierre," says Maude, pointing at Burnaby's Number 10. "I hear she's on the junior national swim team." Kelly is roughly the same height as Jane, but her shoulders are much broader.

"Hmmm," replies Ashley, letting out a big yawn.

Ashley bounces her leg up and down nervously. The white fabric of her uniform shorts stands out against her brown skin. She can't wait to get on the court.

The referee throws the ball up for the tip-off. Jane and Kelly both jump, but Kelly manages to get her palm on the ball first and tips it to her teammate. Surprised by losing the jump ball, Jane hesitates before retreating to defence. Kelly takes advantage of Jane's delay and charges toward the hoop. Her Burnaby teammate passes her the ball, and she scores an easy layup.

Vancouver gets the ball. Scotty confidently dribbles up the right side of the court. She waits for her teammates to get open, but the Burnaby defence is aggressive. No one on Vancouver is open.

"Ten!" yells Ashley to signal that there are only ten seconds remaining on the shot clock. The bench players begin to count down. "Nine, eight, seven . . ."

Scotty waves for all the offensive players to retreat to the baseline. "1–4!" she yells.

Scotty takes two hard dribbles to the right. Her defender lunges to steal the ball, but Scotty crosses the ball behind her back and goes in the other direction.

"Four, three . . ." yells Ashley.

Scotty charges toward the hoop on the left side of the rim, but shoots the ball with her right hand. Suddenly, Kelly leaves her check to challenge Scotty's shot. Without her body to protect the ball, Scotty can't stop Kelly from getting her hand on the ball and swatting it out of bounds.

The referee blows the whistle.

"That's why you need to shoot with your left hand!" yells Coach Catherine.

Scotty takes the ball out of bounds. Because the ball didn't touch the rim, there is only one second remaining on the shot clock. Scotty looks right at Paige, but at the last moment, she softly passes the ball to Leanne underneath the hoop. Again, Kelly rushes to challenge the shot. Spooked by Kelly's presence, Leanne misses the rim.

The shot clock horn sounds and the referee blows the whistle. "Shot clock violation."

Burnaby is awarded the ball.

The game continues. Kelly is the centre of the Burnaby team's offence. Each time down the court, she touches the ball. Each time, Jane struggles to defend her. Jane either gets too aggressive, allowing Kelly to score, or she plays too passively and Kelly makes a great pass to a teammate. By two minutes into the second quarter, Burnaby leads by ten points.

"Ashley!" yells Coach Catherine from the head of the bench. "I want you to sub in for Paige, and I want you checking Number 10."

"Got it," says Ashley, thrilled to play for the first time. "Wait. Number 10?"

Ashley looks out at the court. Kelly grabs a strong rebound.

I'm going to be guarding the best player on the court.

Ashley walks to the scorer's table to substitute into the game. Her heart pounds in her chest.

8 OUT OF CONTROL

Ashley waits nervously at the scorer's table. As the ball zips around the court, Ashley's mouth opens into a wide yawn. It feels strange to be tired and nervous at the same time.

Finally, the play stops and the referee blows her whistle.

"Paige, I've got your sub."

Paige jogs off the court. "I've got Number 13."

Ashley finds Jane. "Jane, you've got Number 13. Coach Catherine wants me to take 10."

"Finally," says Jane. "Now, I can really get going on offence." She looks right at Kelly. Kelly simply shrugs and looks away.

Ashley lines up behind Kelly. The Burnaby team passes the ball to Jane's check. Confident she can defend her new check, Jane lunges at the ball. Number 13 drives toward the basket. As the only Vancouver player near the ball, Ashley steps in to help. She jumps to challenge Number 13's shot, but misses and slaps her wrist.

The referee blows her whistle. "Foul on Vancouver Number 10."

A foul is not how Ashley wanted to start her first game.

"Not your fault, Ashley," says Stephanie from the bench. "Keep playing tough defence."

Number 13 scores both her free throws. Burnaby leads by 12. Ashley takes the ball out of bounds and passes it to Scotty.

"Run!" yells Scotty to the Vancouver team.

"I'm open!" responds Jane. Scotty looks to her then looks away.

Scotty charges full speed up the right-handed side of the court. She looks directly at Paige. The Burnaby defenders jump toward Paige.

"I'm open!" yells Jane.

Scotty ignores her. She takes another hard right-handed dribble toward Paige.

"HERE!" shouts Jane.

Paige's defender's eyes go wide as Scotty approaches. Then, when it looks like Scotty is going to release the ball into Paige's defender's hand, she flips it behind her back and passes it to Jane. Two Burnaby players jump toward her. Jane shoots the ball.

The referee blows the whistle. "Burnaby foul!"

The ball falls through the hoop. Jane pumps her fist.

Jane scores her free throw, cutting the Burnaby lead to 9.

Right away, the Burnaby team charges down the court. Kelly catches the ball at the top of the key.

"Just keep her in front of you, Ashley!" yells Stephanie from the bench.

Ashley shifts her weight to the balls of her feet. Kelly takes a hard dribble to the right, but Ashley slides with her. Kelly is forced to pass the ball away. On the other side of the court, a Burnaby player shoots and misses. Jane gets the rebound and passes it to Scotty who passes it up court to Brea who scores an easy basket. The Burnaby lead is a mere seven points.

Kelly lines up on the wing and waits for her point guard to bring up the ball. The Burnaby point guard throws an off-balance pass in Kelly's direction. Ashley lunges forward and tips the ball away. One step ahead of Kelly, she chases after the ball and runs toward the hoop. Ashley shoots a wide-open right-handed layup. The moment the ball falls through the net, a burst of excitement fills her chest.

I scored my first shot!

"Timeout!" yells the Burnaby coach.

The referee blows her whistle to signal the timeout. Both teams return to their benches. Ashley tries to catch her breath.

"Great work, girls! We need to keep up that defensive intensity!" encourages Coach Catherine.

When the timeout is over, the Burnaby team inbounds the ball. This time, Kelly lines up near the basket again. Kelly is as strong as she is tall, and Ashley's legs are tired from the morning newspaper route. When Jane's check receives the ball, she immediately passes to Kelly, who makes a hard move to the basket. Ashley can do nothing to stop her, and she scores.

"At least challenge her," Jane growls.

"Easy for you to say," Ashley says under her breath. She runs to retrieve the ball out of bounds. But, when Ashley looks out at the court, the Burnaby players are no longer waiting on the defensive side of the court. Instead, they are matched up with their checks in the full court. Caught off guard, Scotty is unable to get open. With the referee counting down, Ashley looks around. No one is open.

"Here!" yells Jane.

Ashley doesn't have time to look and see if Jane's open. She passes the basketball to Jane, but Kelly swoops in front of her and steals it. She scores an easy two points.

Jane looks at Ashley. "You're making her look like the best player in the gym." She drops her voice to a whisper. "Come on, Sneakers. Play like you deserve to be on the team. Or can't you run in those ugly kicks?"

The moment Ashley hears the word "Sneakers," she feels the same anger she felt in practice. But this time, it doesn't have time to turn into hurt.

Before she can stop herself, Ashley shouts, "Shut up, Jane!" as Jane passes the Vancouver bench.

Ugly Kicks

Stephanie and Coach Catherine hear Ashley. Frowning, Coach Catherine substitutes Paige into the game to replace Ashley. Ashley gives Paige a high-five and then clenches her fists as she returns to her spot at the end of the bench.

A few moments later, Coach Catherine comes down to the end of the bench. "You can't yell at teammates on the court."

"I know," says Ashley. "I'm sorry."

"Did Jane say or do something I should know about?"

"She . . ." Ashley catches herself. If she tells Coach Catherine about Jane calling her "Sneakers," Coach Catherine might ask why the nickname bothers her so much. "Not really."

"Okay," says Coach Catherine. "Well, I'm not going to play you for the rest of the game."

Ashley's heart sinks. She barely hears Coach Catherine go on. "It's important to learn how to communicate appropriately with teammates. But, once the game is over, so is your punishment. You'll get another chance next game. Learn from today and move on."

"Okay," says Ashley.

Why did I get so angry?

Ashley hears Jane's words over and over in her head. *"Come on, Sneakers! . . . Come on, Sneakers! . . . Come on, Sneakers!"*

Tears well in Ashley's eyes. She tries to focus on the

game. On the court, Scotty receives the ball and tries to charge up the right side of the court, but her defender's body is directly in her path.

"Go left!" hollers Stephanie.

Scotty nods, but her left hand is still weaker than her right. She struggles to bring the ball up the court.

"You got this!" cheers Ashley. Even if she can't play, she has to keep supporting the team from the bench.

But Vancouver ends up losing by twenty points.

After the game, Coach Catherine says, "Obviously, that's not the score we wanted, but there's a lot we can learn. Hopefully, we'll meet them again in the Provincial Tournament."

"Can we still make the Tier One Tournament?" asks Jane.

"Absolutely," replies Coach Catherine. "We just need to win our next two games."

With the game finished, tears form beneath Ashley's eyelids. She doesn't remember ever feeling as out of control as she was during the game.

Why did I get so mad? Will Coach Catherine really give me another chance?

Ashley tries to make eye contact with Stephanie, hoping to ask her for a ride home. But, Stephanie is on her phone, and then looking into the stands. Ashley follows her gaze. A cute boy with brown hair stands in the bleachers and waves. Stephanie blushes slightly and walks toward him.

Ashley walks up the stairs from the gym and goes into the washroom. The tears welling in her eyes start to fall down her cheeks.

The washroom door swings open. It's Scotty. Ashley madly wipes her cheeks.

Scotty stares at Ashley for a moment. "You okay?"

"Not really." Scotty walks toward the mirror and starts applying her neon-blue eyeliner. "Can I ask you something?"

"You just did."

"It's really annoying when you answer like that."

"Deal with it. What was your question?"

"Why do you wear your makeup like that?"

"I like it."

"And, it never smudges or gets in your eyes?"

"The stuff I don't have to take off is waterproof, smudge-proof, and melt-proof."

"Melt-proof?"

"I could take a trip to the sun, and my eyelashes would still look amazing." Scotty brushes a layer of sparkles onto her cheekbones. "It sucks you got benched today."

"It was my fault. I just . . . I don't get Jane. She's so different off the court."

"She's the same all the time," replies Scotty.

"What do you mean?"

"Watch her closely. You'll see."

9 COUNTING TO TEN

Ashley sits at her desk. She can see Mrs. Hood's mouth move. She can even hear the sounds Mrs. Hood's mouth is making, but nothing is making sense.

"You okay?" whispers Tamara. "That's like the eighth time you've yawned."

"You're counting?" Ashley whispers back.

"It's math class," grins Tamara. "I'm supposed to count things. Seriously though, you okay?"

"I'm fine. I was just up super early for my paper route."

"I'm going to hand back last week's math quiz," announces Mrs. Hood. The class groans. "If you're having trouble with any of the concepts, you're always welcome to come get extra help at lunch or after school." She begins passing back the tests. "Once you've received your quiz, you can leave."

Beside Ashley, Tanya smiles brightly when she looks at her quiz. Ashley nervously flips over her test. Her mark is 11/20.

"Whoa," says Tamara, looking over Ashley's shoulder. "Just eleven. That's really low for you."

"I don't know what happened," mumbles Ashley. But, she knows that isn't totally true. Between basketball, the newspaper route, and babysitting, there hasn't been a lot of time for studying.

"You'll do better next time," says Tanya brightly as they leave the classroom. "Do you want to come over after track practice?"

"I can't," says Ashley without thinking.

"But the countdown is on," whines Tanya. "Wade's gonna be Number 1 this week. I just know it."

"We-e-ell, I could try and come by after practice, but —"

"Awesome!"

"I might be too tired," says Ashley under her breath. But Tanya has already bounced off to her locker.

★★★

Ashley's arms and legs heavy feel heavy as she walks into the gym. She sits behind Maude and Paige.

"New kicks?" asks Paige, nodding at Maude's feet. Her basketball shoes are bright yellow.

"Yeah," replies Maude. "They're a little bright, but they fit like slippers."

"Sweet."

"Hey, Jane," says Paige, looking past Ashley's

shoulder. Jane hops down the steps to join the girls. Ashley feels butterflies flapping in her stomach. Will Jane be mad that Ashley yelled at her during the game?

Why do I care so much what Jane thinks?

"Check out Maude's new shoes," says Paige. Maude beams.

Jane looks down her nose at Maude's shoes. "They're all right, I guess."

"All right? They're totally sweet. They might even be nicer than yours."

Suddenly, Jane's eyes narrow. She cocks her hip to the side, and Ashley feels a tingle run down her spine.

"Nicer than mine?" sneers Jane. "They're road-sign yellow."

"They're a little bright," says Maude shyly. "But I like them."

"Yeah, well, if our team gets lost in a snowstorm, you'll be the first one they find," says Jane with a mean laugh. Some of the players join in, and Maude drops her eyes.

"How do they feel, Maude?" Scotty asks suddenly.

"What?" Maude looks up again.

"How do the shoes feel on your feet?"

"They're . . . perfect."

"So, what's it matter what they look like?"

"Scotty, you're so uncool. You *would* say that," says Jane.

Unlike Maude, Scotty looks Jane square in the eyes. "Yeah, I would."

It must be because Ashley is tired, but for a moment, to her, Scotty seems bigger than she is, and Jane looks much smaller.

"Let's go shoot," says Paige, breaking the tension.

Maude, Paige, and Jane walk to the court.

"That was nice of you," says Ashley to Scotty.

"What?"

"Standing up to Jane."

"I didn't stand up to anyone," says Scotty, blushing slightly.

"You totally did."

"Fine, maybe I did. But only a little."

"So, really, you're like that chocolate bar that's hard on the outside, soft and gooey on the inside."

"You did not just compare me to a chocolate bar."

"Someone has to," Ashley teases. The two girls walk down to the court together. As they grab basketballs from the bin, Ashley sees Jane watching them. Ashley feels herself stepping away from Scotty.

What am I doing?

Ashley grabs a ball. Most of the players are chatting and shooting around at the closest hoop. Scotty glances at the packed hoop and walks to the other end. Ashley follows her.

After practice, Ashley takes the bus to the twins' house.

"Ash!" says Tanya, when Ashley walks through the door. "You're just in time for the music countdown!"

"Just what you were hoping for," says Tamara slyly. "You look sweaty. How was basketball?"

"Meh." Ashley tells the twins all about Jane, Scotty, and Coach Catherine. She leaves out the part about Jane calling her "Sneakers" but gives lots of other details.

"So, this Scotty, does she really have melt-proof mascara?" asks Tanya the instant Ashley finishes.

"I think so?"

"And, her hair's purple, but it's not faded. It's still bright?"

"Yeah," says Ashley. *What is Tanya getting at?*

"I think you're missing the point, Tanya," says Tamara.

"No, *you're* missing the point," says Tanya. "This girl has quality cosmetic products. I want to know where she shops."

"Sometimes, I can't believe you're my sister," says Tamara, rolling her eyes.

"Your twin!" adds Tanya brightly.

Tamara turns to Ashley. "Jane sounds like a bully, Ash."

"She's not," sighs Ashley. "She doesn't say anything super bad, and it's not like I can't stand up for myself. She's just mean on the court. I need to react better."

"Hold on!" says Tanya suddenly. "What?"

"Wade video." Tanya immediately turns up the

volume. If Tamara and Ashley want to keep talking, they'll have to shout over the music. So they turn to watch. On the screen, Wade wanders through an alley, strumming his guitar and running his hands through his hair. Normally, Ashley would hum along, but tonight, she's annoyed by the song's repetitive lyrics.

"Count to ten," says Tanya when the song ends.

"What?" shouts Ashley over the TV.

Tanya turns down the volume. "Count to ten. That's what I do when Tamara makes me mad."

"When do I ever make you mad?" asks Tamara.

There is a moment of silence. Finally, Tanya answers. "Sometimes." She turns to Ashley. "See! I just did it. I counted to ten in my head before I answered, so I wouldn't be mean."

"You just count to ten in your head?" asks Ashley skeptically. "That's it?"

"Dad told me to try it when I get upset. He said it would give me time to think before I react. And, it does. You should try it!"

How am I supposed to count to ten while playing basketball?

As the twins lie back and watch the rest of the countdown, Ashley bounces her knee up and down nervously.

If I want to be on the court, I have stay in control. Maybe I should try counting to ten?

10 COLLISION COURSE

On Monday, Ashley walks through her front door at 7:45 a.m. with her empty newspaper trolley.

"Morning, Ash!" says her mom, pulling Ashley into a hug. "How was the paper route?"

"Fine."

"Just fine?"

"I'm not very good at mornings," admits Ashley.

"Well, if it's too much —"

"No," says Ashley quickly. "It's fine."

"How are you feeling about the big round robin win against Richmond yesterday?"

"Good."

"I'm glad I got to see you play."

"Me too."

"You've got practice tonight, don't you?"

Ashley nods. Her mom furrows her brow. "With the game yesterday, you haven't had a day off."

"It's okay," says Ashley, yawning.

"Well, make sure you pack a good lunch. There's

leftover kaldereta in the fridge."

"Really?!" Ashley opens the fridge door and takes out a plastic container. She opens the lid and sees the cold chicken, potatoes, and peppers covered in tomato sauce. Her mouth begins to water at the sight of her favourite Filipino dish.

"Sweetie, can you help me find my keys?" asks Ashley's mother. Ashley sees that the kitchen table is piled with paper, mail, and garbage. Her mom sighs as she lifts an empty pop can. "Your brother hasn't been doing his chores."

"He'd have to leave his room first," grumbles Ashley.

"Yes, that would be helpful."

Ashley bends to the floor and looks at the linoleum. From the film on the floor, Ashley wonders if Matt's ever actually mopped it. "Found them!"

"Great!" Ashley's mom looks at her keys. The keys are covered in dust and a strand of hair is wrapped around the keychain. "I'll have to clean the kitchen later."

"But, today's a Monday," protests Ashley. "You work two shifts."

"Well, this is our home, and your brother won't do it."

"I'll talk to him."

"You can try." She looks at the clock over the stove. "I've got to go. Love you!"

Ashley looks at her homework sitting on the living

room table. She looks at the clock. If she doesn't do her homework, there's enough time to clean the kitchen before going to school. Ashley opens the cupboard under the kitchen sink, grabs a garbage bag, a pair of gloves, and a cloth, and begins cleaning.

Forty-five minutes later, the kitchen doesn't sparkle like it would on a TV ad, but it looks far better than it did before. As Ashley is packing her lunch and her homework into her bag, her brother wanders into the kitchen.

Matt groggily says, "Something's different. Is it . . . cleaner?"

"You're welcome," grumbles Ashley as she slams the door on her way out.

By lunchtime, Ashley is yawning every two minutes. She wants nothing more than to take a nap during the break, but she has to study for her math quiz.

Tamara asks chirpily, "Coming to the track meeting?"

"I'm not on the track team."

"But we never see you anymore."

"I can't."

"Why not? We can share our lunches!"

Ashley thinks about babysitting, the paper route, her upcoming basketball game, and the math homework she hasn't done. "I just can't!" she snaps.

There's a long silence. "Okay."

Ashley knows she shouldn't have yelled, but she's

too tired to apologize. "I'm going to do my homework in the library. I'll see you in class," she says shortly.

★★★

Midway through Friday's basketball practice, Coach Catherine calls the girls to centre court. "We're going to scrimmage. Ashley, Scotty, Maude, Leanne, and Paige on one team and everyone else on the other."

"Nice," says Maude, giving everyone on her team a high-five. Ashley offers her palm to Maude, but she is too tired to put much energy into slapping Maude's palm.

"Ash, that was the weakest high-five ever," says Maude.

"Sorry," says Ashley.

Why does everything about basketball have to be so hard?

"We're going to work on our fast break," begins Coach Catherine. "The offensive team has ten seconds to get the ball down the floor and shoot. If Stephanie blows the whistle, you've gone over time, and you have to put the ball down where you are. Then, the defensive team will pick up the ball and go on offence."

Ashley's team stands together.

"Who does everyone want to defend?" asks Maude. "I don't want to check Jane. She's too good for me." She turns to Ashley. "Do you want to take her?"

"Not really," says Ashley, looking across the court at Jane. "But I could."

"Great!" says Maude. The rest of the girls decide on their checks and then line up at the centre circle for tip-off.

Jane stands in the centre circle, but no one from Ashley's team stands across from her.

"Paige, you're the tallest," says Ashley. "You should take the tip-off."

"You're her check," argues Paige. "You should do it."

Ashley grumbles but stands across from Jane. Coach Catherine throws the ball in the air. Ashley and Jane both jump. Jane easily tips it to her teammate who passes the ball up the court to Jocelyn. Jocelyn shoots an off-balance shot. Paige gets the rebound.

"Don't rush your shot," instructs Stephanie from the sideline.

"Here," says Scotty, signalling to Paige to pass her the ball. When Scotty receives the ball, she looks up court. Faster than Jane, Ashley's able to get a step ahead of her. Scotty looks away from Ashley, but shouts, "Keep going, Ash!" Ashley does as she's told and runs hard to the basket. Because Scotty is looking in the other direction, Jane cheats away from Ashley, leaving her wide open. Suddenly, Scotty releases the ball. Her pass is perfect, landing right in Ashley's hands, but Ashley bobbles the pass and it goes out of bounds. "Nice pass, Scotty," says Stephanie from the sideline. "Focus on the catch, Ashley."

"Jane," shouts Coach Catherine, "don't lose your check."

Jane nods and runs in the opposite direction. Ashley sprints to get between Jane and the basket. As Brea passes the ball to Jane, Ashley plants her back foot and changes direction. She lunges toward the ball, but her legs are slow and tired and she misses. The ball bounces out of bounds.

"Brea's team's ball," instructs Coach Catherine.

"Nice move, Ash," says Maude.

"Lucky," says Jane under her breath.

Ashley's first instinct is to react, but she stops herself. Under her breath, Ashley begins to count, "one, two, three, four . . ."

Suddenly, the ball is being passed inbounds to Jane. Ashley is a step behind and Jane scores an easy layup. Jane looks over her shoulder at Ashley.

"What are you looking at?" says Ashley as Jane brushes past her.

Jane doesn't answer. She just runs up the court with a smug smile, and the expression on Jane's face causes the frustration Ashley feels to boil into anger.

"Keep playing," instructs Scotty, as she catches the ball.

"Right," says Ashley under her breath. Scotty surveys the court. Her eyes seem to focus on the ball instead of the court, so Brea lunges to steal the ball. But Scotty dribbles the ball behind her back and explodes past Brea. Maude's defender steps in to stop Scotty, and the moment she moves, Scotty has passed the ball to Maude for an easy shot.

Ashley hustles back to play defence, racing to keep up with Jane's long strides. She manages to beat Jane down the court, and keep her body between Jane and the hoop.

"Here!" yells Jane, signalling she wants the ball.

Brea looks at Jane and then at Ashley. "Not open."

Jane cuts toward the basket, bumping into Ashley and forcing her backwards.

"Watch it!" says Ashley.

"Here!" yells Jane to Brea again. Brea hesitates, and it gives Ashley just enough time to regain her balance and lunge forward to tip away the ball. At the same moment, Jane steps toward the ball.

Thwack!

The next thing Ashley knows, she's on the ground beside Jane.

11 CLEAN UP

Stephanie's whistle blows. "Everyone all right?"

Ashley's elbow is a little sore from the sudden landing, but otherwise, nothing hurts.

"You did that on purpose!" accuses Jane.

"I was going for the ball."

"Whatever, Sneakers."

"What did you just call me?"

"Girls?" calls Coach Catherine from the sideline.

"They're fine, Coach," says Scotty quickly. She looks at Jane and Ashley. "If you two don't cool it, we're all going to get in trouble." She holds out her hands. Jane rolls away from Scotty, but Ashley accepts Scotty's outstretched palm.

Scotty tugs Ashley to her feet. "You can't let her get to you, Ash."

"I know," says Ashley sharply.

Ashley watches Jane as she casually drinks from her water bottle, but she can't stop thinking about the collision. She remembers the moment Brea released the ball to pass it up court to Jane. She remembers lunging to tip the ball away.

I totally was going for the ball! Jane is crazy.

In the next scrimmage, Ashley switches checks with Paige. With Jane on the opposite side of the court, there are no more incidents, but Ashley still can't shake her thoughts. She remembers the moment Brea released the ball to pass it up court to Jane. She remembers lunging to tip the ball away.

I totally was going for the ball!

Jane's words echo in her mind:

"You did that on purpose . . . Whatever, Sneakers. You did that on purpose . . . Whatever, Sneakers. You did that on purpose . . . Whatever, Sneakers."

Ashley looks at Jane who is chatting with Maude. *Ugh!*

Ashley spends the rest of practice wishing her heavy legs were standing anywhere but on a basketball court.

"Tomorrow, we've got our final round robin game," says Coach Catherine as the players stretch. "If we win, we'll qualify for the Tier One Tournament. Make sure to get your rest between now and the game."

"Ash," says Stephanie. She waves at Ashley. "Hey, can you hang back for a second?"

"Yeah?"

"Your next installment for the fee is due today," says Stephanie carefully. "Do you have it?"

"It's in my bag," sighs Ashley. "I should've given it to

you at the beginning of practice. Sorry."

"It's okay," Stephanie says gently. She pauses. "You didn't look like yourself out on the court today. Is everything all right?"

"Sorry," Ashley says again.

"What for?"

"Bobbling the ball. Being slow on defence. Generally sucking."

"Hey," interrupts Stephanie instantly. "Don't be so negative. Did you mean to bobble the ball?"

"No."

"So, why would you be sorry?"

"I don't know."

"Do you want to talk about it?"

"There's nothing to talk about," says Ashley shortly. "I'm just tired."

"Okay, well, get lots of rest before tomorrow, and if you ever do want to talk, let me know."

"I will. Can I get a ride home?"

"Sorry, I've got plans tonight." Stephanie looks to the top of the bleachers. The handsome boy waves.

"It's all right. I can catch the bus."

Stephanie tilts her head to the side sympathetically. "Let me see if Paige's mom can give you a ride."

Ten minutes later, Ashley is sitting in the back of Paige's car.

"I'm super stoked for tomorrow's game," says Paige. "I'm going to relax tonight so I'm ready."

"Yeah," replies Ashley, half-heartedly. Her muscles ache and mind feels fuzzy. "I just want to go to bed."

"Maybe I'll watch a rerun of the countdown," adds Paige casually.

"I miss the countdown."

Ashley reaches into her bag, pulls out her phone, and dials Tanya's number. The phone rings, but there is no answer. She dials Tamara's number. Again, no answer.

"We're here," says Paige's mom, stopping in front of Ashley's apartment.

"Thanks for the ride," says Ashley.

"Anytime," replies Paige's mom. "Have a good night, Ashley."

★★★

Ashley opens the apartment door and plops her backpack down on the ground.

"Did Stephanie drive you home?" asks Matt, suddenly popping up from his spot on the couch.

"No. I got a ride with Paige."

"Why?" asks Matt, but before Ashley can answer, he continues. "Did she tell you about her date?"

"She has a date? Is it that cute guy she talks to after our games?"

"He's not cute. And why didn't you tell me about him?!" Matt demands.

"There was nothing to tell."

"Obviously, there was. You remember him."

"Why do you care?"

Matt looks away suddenly. "I don't."

"Oh . . ." says Ashley, thinking aloud. "You like her."

Matt's face goes bright red. "You're just like everyone else. You know nothing about me. Nothing!" With that, Matt stomps out of the living room, down the hall, and slams his bedroom door.

★★★

On Saturday morning, it is pouring rain and Ashley is soaked to the bone. She drags the empty newspaper trolley behind her. After parking the trolley in the family's storage locker at the back of the apartment building, Ashley walks down the apartment building hallway.

Looking forward to a shower and a nap, Ashley opens the apartment door. Her mom is standing completely still in the middle of the living room.

"Mom? Is everything okay?" asks Ashley tentatively.

"Your brother is supposed to clean up after himself. It looks like his backpack exploded in here. I was going to clean, but I don't even know where to start. And now it's time for work."

"I'll talk to him," says Ashley.

Ashley's mom hesitates. "He doesn't yell at you when you ask, does he?"

Clean Up

"Nope," says Ashley, not adding that he doesn't yell because she doesn't ask.

"Well, that did seem to work last time." Ashley's mom steps gingerly out of the mess. "Good luck in your game today. It's a big one, right?"

"Yeah," says Ashley, yawning. "If we win, we go to the Tier One Tournament, and if we lose, we'll be in the Tier Two Tournament."

"I'll be thinking of you and cheering while I'm at work."

After a hug, Ashley's mom leaves. Ashley looks at the living room. Then, she looks at the clock. If she cleans, there won't be time for either a nap or a shower.

Ashley sighs, goes to the kitchen, and gets cleaning supplies.

12 LOSING IT

"Vancouver!" cheers Ashley's team.

At the other bench, Fraser Valley also cheers. The starting line-ups for both teams walk onto the court. Ashley takes her seat on the bench beside Maude.

"I really want to win this game and go to Victoria for the Tier One Tournament," says Maude.

"Yeah," mutters Ashley. Her mind feels like a swamp. Everything is smoggy and mucky. Why are her legs so sore? Why is her hair still wet from delivering papers in the rain?

On the court, the game begins. The Fraser Valley Regional team wears bright green uniforms. Jane wins the jump ball and tips it. Scotty grabs it and immediately passes the ball up court to Leanne. Leanne scores!

"Good start!" yells Maude.

Fraser Valley charges up the court. Their point guard passes the ball up court to Number 7 outside the three-point line. As soon as Number 7 touches the ball, she shoots and scores a three-point shot.

Losing It

Fraser Valley plays an aggressive style of defence. Scotty has to work extra hard to dribble the ball up court. When she crosses half, she signals for everyone to retreat to the baseline to run 1–4. With the shot clock counting down, Scotty drives hard to her right. She scores.

Fraser Valley responds. They pass the ball up court to Number 7 outside the three-point line. She shoots and scores a three-point shot.

"Ashley!" yells Coach Catherine. It's the first time Ashley has been called into the game before the second quarter. Ashley jogs toward the scorer's table. "Sub in for Paige. I want you to defend Number 7."

"Don't give her any room to shoot," instructs Stephanie.

Like Burnaby, the Fraser Valley team is forcing Scotty to dribble with her left hand. Scotty passes the ball to Ashley. Exhausted, Ashley bobbles the pass, and Number 7 aggressively swats the ball out of her hands and out of bounds.

"Sorry," says Ashley to Scotty.

"Be strong with the ball, Ashley," instructs Coach Catherine from the bench.

As Scotty walks past Ashley, she says, "I'm going to pass to you again. Catch the ball, hold onto it like Jane's trying to rip it from your hands, and wait for me to cut. Got it?"

Ashley nods. Paige takes the ball from the referee and passes it inbounds to Scotty. Scotty waits for everyone to get in their offensive spots. Ashley doesn't really want the ball again so soon after making a mistake, but Scotty is looking to her side of the court. Ashley cuts to get open. Scotty passes her the ball. Number 7 goes to intercept the pass, but Ashley reaches out. She feels slow and foggy, like she's playing in a swamp. The ball touches her hands, and a jolt of panic rushes through her body.

I'm going to drop the pass again.

"Rip it!" hollers Scotty.

Ashley controls the ball and rips it across her body to her right hip. She waits. Scotty looks away, and Ashley can feel her heart thump in her chest. Suddenly, Scotty charges at the basket. Ashley passes her the ball. It's wobbly and off-target, but Scotty manages to catch the basketball and shoot all in one motion. She scores.

"Nice pass, Ash," says Scotty.

Ashley hustles back on defence. Number 7 is quick. Ashley has to concentrate and stay close to her. Jane's check receives the ball on the wing. She passes the ball to Number 7. Ashley keeps her arm outstretched and her weight on the balls of her feet. Number 7 looks at the rim, but decides not to shoot. She passes the ball away.

"Good work, Ashley," encourages Stephanie from the bench.

Ashley plays the rest of the first quarter. It's far more minutes than she's used to. Ashley struggles to catch her breath as she jogs to the bench.

Coach Catherine talks to the team. "Scotty is doing a great job of bringing the ball up the court, but everyone needs to work harder to get open for her. Ashley, I want you to start the second quarter. Keep guarding Number 7."

When the referee blows the whistle to signal the end of quarter time, Ashley has barely caught her breath.

The Fraser Valley team begins on offence. Their point guard passes the ball to Number 7. Ashley keeps her arm extended to discourage Number 7 from shooting. Number 7 looks at the rim, but, again, decides to pass the ball away.

The Fraser Valley Coach yells, "Joan, you've got to look to score."

"She's right in my face," mumbles Joan under her breath.

On the other side of the court, a Fraser Valley player shoots and scores.

Under extreme pressure from her defender, Scotty dribbles up court. Ashley takes two hard steps to the basket. Her defender doesn't follow. Before Ashley has time to process that she's open, Scotty passes her the ball. Ashley catches the ball wide open under the rim. But, in her fog, she struggles to find her balance. She throws a shot at the rim and misses. The rebound bounces out of bounds.

"Good cut," encourages Scotty.

"Terrible shot," mumbles Ashley.

Ashley sprints back on defence. The moment Ashley gets in defensive stance, Number 7 receives the ball. She looks Ashley square in the eyes and shoots. Caught off-guard, Ashley can do nothing but watch the ball sail through the air toward the hoop. Luckily, the shot is short and hard. It clanks off the rim and soars directly out of bounds.

"You can't let her shoot," says Jane to Ashley as they wait for the referee to retrieve the ball from the corner of the gym. "Wake up, Sneakers."

"Sneakers?" asks Number 7. She looks down at Ashley's shoes. "I get it. It's because your kicks are so ugly. Right?" she taunts.

Ashley shoots Jane a glare. To her surprise, Jane's expression is like a kid caught with their hand in the cookie jar.

"Shut up," sneers Ashley under her breath before she can stop herself.

Number 7's voice sticks in Ashley's mind: *"Your kicks are so ugly."*

Ashley's stomach clenches and her body aches, but she tries to focus. Vancouver has to win this game.

By the fourth quarter, Vancouver leads Fraser Valley by seven points. Ashley's defence has severely limited Number 7's scoring chances. As the game nears its end, the play gets even more intense.

When Number 7 receives the ball on the wing, her coach shouts, "Look to score!"

Ashley keeps her arm outstretched. Number 7 fakes the shot, but Ashley doesn't move. Expecting her fake to work, Number 7 drives at Ashley. Ashley jumps backward, but Number 7 slams into her chest, knocking Ashley to the ground.

The referee blows her whistle. "Foul on Vancouver Number 10."

"What?" Ashley says from the ground. Scotty runs over to help her up.

"Your feet were moving," says the referee.

"That's a terrible call," complains Coach Catherine from the bench.

"But she knocked me over," Ashley says to Scotty.

"Deal with it, Sneakers," snarls Number 7.

Ashley stands to confront Number 7, but Scotty doesn't let go of her hand, pulling Ashley away from the scene.

Ashley rips her wrist away from Scotty's grip. "What are you doing?"

"Calm down," says Scotty seriously. "We need you in the game if we're going to win. The best way to get her back is to beat her."

Ashley marches to the key. Number 7 makes her first free throw. She takes the ball for her second free throw. As she releases the ball, Ashley can tell the shot is going to miss to the right of the rim. Immediately, Ashley moves to chase after the ball, but a Fraser Valley player gets there first. Number 7 has cut toward the basket and is wide open. In the back of Ashley's mind, she knows that it's too late to intercept the pass. But, all Ashley can think of is stopping Number 7 from scoring.

Ashley plants her foot and lunges for the ball. At the same moment, Number 7 reaches for the ball. Ashley jumps into the air. Her fingertip grazes the ball, but she's too far away to change its path. Number 7 catches the ball and scores. As Ashley lands, her tired leg buckles. Her foot rolls underneath her ankle and she falls to the ground. Ashley feels pain shoot through her leg.

"Agh!" yells Ashley. Tears well in her eyes. The referee blows her whistle, and the teams gather at their benches.

Stephanie jogs over to Ashley, who is alone on the court. "Are you okay? What hurts?"

"My ankle," sniffles Ashley.

Stephanie bends to take a look. When she tenderly touches Ashley's ankle, Ashley feels another burst of pain.

With Stephanie's help, Ashley gets up off the ground and hops to the end of the bench. Stephanie makes Ashley sit on the floor with her foot resting on the bench. Carefully, Stephanie removes Ashley's shoe and sock, secures her ankle with athletic tape, and puts ice over top of the swollen area. All Ashley can do is sit and cry.

On the court, Number 7 starts to find her groove. She shoots three-point shots. She drives to the hoop. But, Vancouver keeps the game close. With fifteen seconds left to play, the game is tied. Coach Catherine calls a timeout.

"We're going to run 1–4," says Coach Catherine. She looks at Scotty. "Beat your check. If no one comes to help, shoot. Otherwise, pass it to the open player."

Scotty gulps.

The players run back onto the court. The referee hands Paige the ball out of bounds. She quickly passes it inbounds to Scotty. The game clock begins.

"Ten, nine, eight . . ." yell the Vancouver bench players.

With seven seconds left in the game, Scotty takes a hard dribble to the right, crosses the ball over to her left hand, and then immediately back to her right hand. Her defender gets lost in the moves, and Scotty charges past her. Jane's defender steps in to stop her, and Scotty immediately makes an easy pass to Jane, who scores with no time left on the clock.

Vancouver wins by one point!

The players on the bench jump and run to celebrate with the team. But, with her ankle injury, Ashley is left on the bench alone.

13 SIDELINED

In the locker room after the game, there's a buzz of excitement, but Ashley just sits on the bench while the other players change. Her ankle hurts. Her hair still isn't dry, and she's holding the information sheet for the trip to Victoria.

Coach Catherine handed out the sheets after the game. It's full of words, but Ashley can only see numbers. There is a tournament fee of one hundred dollars. Another hundred dollars is needed for travel and hotel costs. And the organizers suggest that each player bring a hundred for food, souvenirs, and other expenses. As tired as she is, Ashley can do the math: she needs three hundred dollars.

With her ankle sprained, Ashley can't do her paper route. Without her paper route, Ashley won't be able to save enough money to go to the tournament.

Do I even want to play basketball?

A raised voice breaks Ashley from her thoughts. Ashley looks up and sees that everyone but Jane and Scotty have left the locker room.

"If you'd have passed to me earlier, the game never would've gotten that close," Jane growls at Scotty.

Jane's cruel tone rings in Ashley's ears. It's the same tone she uses when she calls Ashley "Sneakers." Before she can stop herself, Ashley speaks up. "Seriously?"

"I wasn't talking to you," Jane says dismissively.

"Well, you're talking to me now." Ashley is furious. "How dare you accuse Scotty of being selfish!"

"I was open the whole game."

"Maybe *she* was open too. Did you ever think of that? And she passed you the ball at the end of the game. When it mattered most."

"Of course she did. I'm the star of this team. The ball should always be in my hands." As soon as the words leave Jane's mouth, her expression drops and she turns bright red. "I mean —"

"You said exactly what you meant," says Ashley.

I can't believe it's taken me this long to see who you really are.

Ashley watches as her words wash over Jane. For a brief moment, there's hurt in Jane's eyes. But, Jane shakes it away. "Whatever." She grabs her bag and goes to the door. Just before she leaves, she turns. "Hope your ankle gets better," Jane sneers. "It would suck if you couldn't come to Victoria with us."

The change room door closes. The anger Ashley felt when Jane was in the room melts away. "I shouldn't have done that."

"Maybe not," shrugs Scotty. "But thanks."

Suddenly, the change room door swings open. A small woman with black hair stands on the other side. "There you are."

"Hi, Mom," replies Scotty.

"If we're going to get to Lisa's piano recital, you need to hurry."

Scotty quickly puts her makeup bag in her backpack and slings it over one shoulder. She offers her hand to Ashley. "Come on. I'll help you get upstairs."

Ashley reaches out and takes Scotty's hand. When she's standing, she leans against Scotty's shoulder and limps out of the change room and up the bleacher stairs. The gym is practically empty, but from the lobby, loud voices echo.

"Fine! You want to know about my date? It was terrible. He was ten minutes late to pick me up. So we missed the previews, and there was no time to get popcorn. Which is basically the best part of going to the movies," says Stephanie. "But I didn't call you to talk about my *date*. I called you so *you* could take care of your *sister*."

"I'm here, aren't I?"

Scotty helps Ashley limp into the lobby where Matt and Stephanie are standing face to face, glaring daggers at each other.

"Well, aren't you a hero?" scoffs Stephanie. Her voice is so shrill that both Ashley and Scotty stop in their tracks. "You are just so generous for offering to give your injured sister a ride home?"

"Well, sorry I can't be as perfect as Max," says Matt mockingly.

"I don't need you to be perfect! I don't need you to play soccer. I don't need you to be the star. I don't even need you to brush you hair." Stephanie takes a deep breath and lowers her voice. "You used to kiss your mom on the cheek before you left the house and come to all my basketball games with a giant sign. You used to ride an extra bus stop to make sure your little sister got to school okay. Where is that guy? Because that's the guy I need, and more importantly, that's the guy your sister needs."

There's a long moment of silence.

Suddenly, Scotty's mom whispers to her. "We've got to go."

Scotty nods, and they quietly walk toward the door. The sound of their footsteps startles Matt and Stephanie from their argument. Stephanie looks over at Ashley. There are tears in her eyes. She turns and walks out of the lobby. Ashley and Matt are left standing alone.

Silence.

"I borrowed a car from Mrs. Greene," says Matt finally. "Mom would've come, but she's stuck at work. Do you need help getting to the car? I could, uh, give you a piggyback?"

"I'll just hop."

Ashley follows Matt to the parking lot in silence. They get into Mrs. Greene's car. There's a tiny heart hanging from the rearview mirror. It's scented like cinnamon, which makes the whole car smell like pie. Matt turns on the car and pulls out of the parking lot.

"How's the ankle?"

"Sore."

"S-so, uh," Matt stammers, "your team made the big tournament?"

"Yup."

"Are you excited?"

"Not really," Ashley says honestly. "Basketball hasn't been very much fun lately, and I probably can't go anyways."

"Why not?"

Ashley doesn't want to hear one of Matt's rants about how much it sucks to be poor. She remembers Jane in the change room. The injury gives her the perfect way out. "Because of my ankle."

"Kind of like me and my knee."

"Guess so."

★★★

Ashley is standing at the three-point line. She is looking up at the score clock. There are thirty seconds left in the game, and the score is 54–54. Ashley's gaze drifts to the bleachers. They're filled with people. All eyes are on the court. Ashley feels excitement pulse through her body.

Scotty comes jogging toward her.

"Ready?" asks Ashley.

"It's the Championship Final. I'd better be ready."

Ashley feels a surge of energy. She's never been in a championship final before. As the referee walks to the sideline with the ball, Ashley gets in defensive stance.

"You think you can stop me?" says her check, Number 7. Her tone is sharp and cruel. "You're kidding yourself, Sneakers."

Before Ashley can stop herself, she's shoving Number 7. The girl falls to the ground. The referee is running toward her with her hands in the "technical foul" gesture. The other team will be awarded two free throws and the ball. This could cost Vancouver the game.

Ashley hears a whistle. Suddenly, the whistle turns into a beeping. A beeping that won't stop.

Ashley sits straight up in bed. She looks around, confused. Then she realizes where she is and turns off her alarm. Her heart is still pounding. She should've known it was a dream. Ashley would never shove someone. Would she? Ashley remembers Saturday's game. She was so mad at Number 7 that she went for the ball even when she knew she couldn't get it.

Ashley rolls out of bed and puts her foot on the ground. It's Monday morning, and for the first time since Saturday, her ankle doesn't throb the moment her foot touches the rug. She slowly limps around her room.

Ashley picks up her phone and dials a number. "Mr. Penumbra?"

"Yes?"

"It's Ashley . . . from the paper route."

"Of course!"

Ashley takes a deep breath. "I've sprained my ankle. I don't think I'm going to be able to deliver papers this week."

"Oh no!" says Mr. Penumbra. Ashley braces herself to be yelled at for letting him down. "Are you all right?"

"Yeah," says Ashley, a little surprised. "But, it's still pretty sore."

"Well, I hope it gets better soon. I'll get someone to cover the route. You take care of yourself. No calling me until you're completely healed, you understand?"

Once she's dressed, Ashley limps to the kitchen. Matt is sitting at the kitchen table, holding a piece of paper.

"You're up," says Ashley. She's amazed to see her brother out of bed well before he has to leave for school.

"You were lying."

"What?"

"About Victoria. Your ankle isn't the reason you might not be able to go." Matt turns over the piece of paper in his hand. It's the information sheet Coach Catherine handed out.

Ashley clenches her jaw. "Where did you get that?"

"I found it on the couch last night."

"Well, it's mine," says Ashley furiously.

"Technically, it's for Mom."

"What's for me?" asks their mom as she bustles into the kitchen.

Matt tucks the sheet behind his back. "Nothing."

Their mother raises an eyebrow. "How's your ankle, Ash?"

"Not great."

"Be careful at school today. Mrs. Greene said we can borrow her car again, so you don't have to walk."

On the ride to school, Ashley thinks about the twins. They still haven't answered any of her calls. They must be furious with her. Will they be at school? Will they ignore her? Will they yell at her? Most importantly, will Ashley get the chance to tell them how sorry she is? By the time she walks down the hallway to her classroom, her stomach is in knots. But when Ashley walks into class, the twins are nowhere to be seen. She sighs.

Mrs. Hood calls the attendance. When she calls Ashley's name, she pauses. Ashley thinks of her quiz scores and her heart sinks. "Ashley, can you please see me at lunch?"

The morning passes slowly, but without waking up early to deliver papers, Ashley notices how much more awake she feels. She's able to focus on Mrs. Hood's lesson and take in all the information. For the first time in weeks, she doesn't feel completely lost in class.

Ashley takes her lunch and goes to the gym. She

gently pulls open the door. The gym is empty and the bleachers are pulled out. Ashley sits down and stares at the floor. She thinks about Saturday's game. Her mind was hazy and her legs felt heavy. She remembers bobbling the ball on the first pass and blushes with embarrassment.

What kind of basketball player can't catch a basketball?

Then Ashley remembers Number 7 calling her "Sneakers." It felt like a flip was switched inside her belly, tossing all her tiredness and anger together until her stomach clenched into a knot. Ashley replays the fourth quarter in her mind. She remembers her tight shoulder muscles, her heavy calves, and her drooping eyelids. Then, she feels the jolt of pain, as she sprains her ankle. She stares out at the empty gym. Isn't basketball supposed to be fun?

Maybe it's a good thing she can't go to Victoria.

14 HELPING HANDS

When Ashley walks through the front door, Matt's in his usual spot on the couch, but he isn't lying down like a sloth. Instead, he's sitting upright, staring at a piece of paper on the coffee table.

"I want to talk to you," he says. Ashley sits in the recliner across from him. Matt runs his hand through his hair. It looks shinier than usual. In fact, Matt looks a little shinier. He's wearing jeans that fit, and a T-shirt Ashley hasn't seen in over a year.

Matt takes a deep breath. "I've had a really bad year."

Ashley expects Matt to continue, but he just leaves the comment hanging. "Because of your knee?"

"It started with my knee. It was like I tore more than just my ligament. Does that make sense?"

"Not really," answers Ashley honestly.

"Soccer was my life, and then suddenly, it wasn't anymore. It's just . . . it's been hard." Matt finally stops looking at the ceiling and looks back at Ashley. "But that doesn't matter now. What matters is that I can help you."

"How?"

"Steph was right: there are things we can't change. Three hundred dollars is a lot of money for our family, but I think you should go to Victoria."

"It's not worth it."

"You don't mean that."

"Actually, I do," says Ashley sharply. "It's too much money, and I just finished paying off my registration fee. Basketball isn't even fun anymore."

There's a long silence. Matt reaches out and touches his knee. "You sound like me."

"Whatever."

"Listen," says Matt seriously. "I get it. I took a second job to help cover the cost of physio, but it was so much work, and I was just . . . tired. It made me not want to play anymore."

That's exactly how I feel.

Matt looks right at Ashley. "But now that I've actually stopped playing soccer, it's different. And, if you quit basketball, it'll be different for you too."

"Why do you suddenly care so much about me and basketball?"

Matt takes a deep breath and holds it for a moment before sighing. "Steph was right . . . about a lot of things. You shouldn't give up on basketball. Not yet."

"We can't afford it."

"I've been brainstorming ways we can cut the costs of your tournament." Ashley looks at the paper. The cost is written in the middle and there are a few squiggly lines leading toward words like "hotel" and "fees," but there isn't much else. "It's hard, but we have to try. What do you say?"

Ashley's not convinced she wants to play that badly, but she can't remember the last time Matt made this much effort for her. For anything. "I guess we can try."

Matt runs his hands through his hair. "We just need to think about things . . . differently. I wish Steph was here. She's so good at this stuff." He looks at the paper again. "Instead of thinking of the costs as a whole . . . let's try and break them up. What can we do to cut the estimated costs you have control of?"

There's a long silence as Ashley and Matt stare at the paper.

"I could bring a cooler with food, so I don't have to pay so much for eating out?"

"That's great!" says Matt.

Matt scribbles "cooler" on the piece of paper.

Matt and Ashley spend the next hour brainstorming ideas. At first, there are lots of awkward pauses and long silences, but it gets more fun as they go. By the time they're done, Ashley has a list of items that she guesses will help her cut down costs.

"What about the fee? I haven't been able to do the paper route because of my ankle but —"

"No," says Matt suddenly. "You've been doing too much. Babysitting is enough."

"It's not enough if I don't have the money."

"I'll see what I can do."

"What's that mean?"

"Exactly what it sounds like," says Matt. "The newspaper route is too much. I'll see what I can do to help with the fee."

Before Ashley can argue, Matt abruptly gets up. "This was good."

"Yeah . . ." says Ashley.

Was Matt actually . . . helpful?

Ashley hears Matt close his bedroom door.

Can I trust him? Will he really help with the fee?

★★★

Ashley limps into the gym and looks down at the court. How will it feel to watch practice and not play? Before Ashley can think too hard, she feels Jane's glare from across the bleachers and a shiver runs through her body.

"How's the ankle?" asks Scotty, startling Ashley from her thoughts.

"Sore," says Ashley. She hesitates. "I don't know if I'm going to be able to come to Victoria."

Scotty's eyes go wide. "Nope."

"What?"

"Get up. We're going to the washroom."

"What? Why?"

"Up." Ashley tentatively stands and moves to start

hopping up the stairs. Before she can move forward, Scotty ducks under Ashley's arm to help support her.

"I can do it myself," complains Ashley.

"You could, but why would you?"

"Hmpf," says Ashley as she leans on Scotty for support.

When they get to the washroom, Scotty immediately checks under the stalls to make sure no one else is in the room. "So, what's this about Victoria?"

"I told you. My ankle's bummed."

"This has nothing to do with what Jane said on Saturday?"

Ashley hesitates. "Not really."

"Not really?"

"Look, you won't get it," says Ashley, frustrated.

"Then help me get it."

"I can't!" Ashley expects Scotty to yell back, but she doesn't. She simply looks at Ashley with a puzzled expression on her face. "Why do you care anyways? It won't hurt the team."

"You're our best defender," says Scotty. "And, if I only cared about winning, I'd be best friends with Jane."

"That would be weird."

"Right?! But, my point is, I care if you're on the team."

"Why?"

Scotty rolls her eyes and takes a deep breath. "Because you're kind of an awesome human. I've been in Jane's class since kindergarten. Do you know how many people have stood up to her?"

"Not very many?"

"Bingo! And you didn't just stand up to her. You stood up for me. No one stands up for me."

"That sucks."

"I can take care of myself," says Scotty, puffing out her chest. "Well . . . mostly. But, I didn't have to on Saturday. Because you were there. You're funny. You work hard. And you've got bite, and I like that. So, yeah, I care if you're not on the team." Ashley lets Scotty's words sink in. How does Scotty see all these things about her? "I get that you don't want to tell me what's going on —"

"It's not that I don't want to tell you," Ashley sighs out. "There's nothing to tell."

"I doubt that."

"I've just been really busy."

"With?"

Ashley sighs again. "Basketball, babysitting, my newspaper route, homework, my chores —"

Scotty's eyes widen in disbelief. "That's a lot."

"I'm not done yet," says Ashley. Seeing the expression on Scotty's face, Ashley realizes just how busy she's been. "I've been doing my brother's chores too, and I've been bombing my quizzes at school. Nothing's been fun. Not even basketball. So maybe it's a good thing I won't be coming to Victoria."

"Hold on. Why on earth would you be doing your brother's chores?"

"It's a long story."

"It'd better be. I'd never do my sister's chores." Scotty pauses and stares intently into space. It reminds Ashley of Scotty's expression while watching the other pairs compete in the shooting game in the second try-out. Suddenly, Scotty snaps her head to look at Ashley. "You're not allowed to touch a basketball at practice today."

"I can't practice anyways because of my ankle."

"I know that, but no touching basketballs either."

"Okay . . ." says Ashley, confused.

"Now, let's get back in there," says Scotty, walking over to Ashley to help her manoeuvre back to the gym.

15 SITTING OUT

Ashley sits on a bench beside the court and watches practice. It begins with a layup drill. The players have to make ten layups in a row. The team easily completes the right-handed layups, but the left-handed layups are another story.

Scotty clanks a left-handed layup off the rim.

"Good effort," says Stephanie.

Scotty just sighs. By the time the team is on their eighth attempt at making ten layups, Scotty still hasn't scored any of her baskets.

"Seven," yells out Jocelyn as she completes her layup.

Scotty is next in line. But, instead of catching the ball when it's passed to her, she suddenly bends to the ground. "Shoelace is untied."

Ashley looks at Scotty's feet. Her shoes are perfectly done up with double bows. Ashley looks at the coaches, who are deep in conversation. They don't notice Scotty's lie.

"Eight!" yells the team as Maude finishes her layup.

Scotty makes sure not to stand until the team finally makes ten layups.

As Ashley watches the practice, she starts to feel something strange. It's a deep feeling, straight from her gut. A ball from a shooting drill bounces toward Ashley, and she feels a jolt of excitement. She gets up off the bench to hop toward it. Suddenly, Scotty sprints toward her.

"Nope," says Scotty. "Remember the rules."

Ashley growls under her breath. "I remember."

Scotty chuckles in response.

Ashley watches the ball zip around the court. She can feel her heart beat with excitement and yearning. She really wants to touch a basketball and be on the court with her teammates. She remembers what Matt said:

"Now that I've actually stopped playing, it's different."

As her teammates play, Ashley wants nothing more than to have a ball in her hand. She closes her eyes and imagines spinning a leather basketball against her palm. With her eyes shut, Ashley lets her mind wander to her conversation with Scotty in the washroom.

Scotty sees Ashley so much differently than she sees herself. Ashley looks out on the court and remembers Saturday's game. Except, this time, Ashley imagines the game as though she was a spectator. Ashley was subbed into the game early. She remembers fumbling Scotty's first pass. From the outside, it isn't embarrassing; it's just an accident. Ashley watches herself recover the next play, and make a pass to Scotty, who scores. Ashley watches herself stop Number 7 on defence. A surge of pride blasts through Ashley's body. As the game goes on, Ashley watches herself get angry and ashamed when Number 7 calls her "Sneakers." She sees herself go after the rebound and sprain her ankle. It all looks so different from the outside.

Coach Catherine blows the whistle to signal the end of practice, and it jolts Ashley from her thoughts. Ashley hops over to the team to cheer with them.

When practice is over, Scotty walks over, spinning a basketball in her palms. Ashley holds out her hands to signal for Scotty to pass her the ball. "Nuh-uh," says Scotty, shaking her head.

"Practice is over," complains Ashley.

"And how did it feel not to play?"

"Not good."

"Still planning not to come to Victoria?"

"It depends on how my ankle's doing," says Ashley, thinking about the fee. Just because Ashley wants to go doesn't mean she'll be able to afford it. She thinks about Matt. He gave up on soccer and he's been unhappy all year. Maybe she shouldn't give up yet. "But I'm going to try."

"I'll take that," says Scotty, finally passing Ashley the ball. Ashley spins the ball in her hand several times. "Feels good, doesn't it?"

"Yeah . . ."

"You don't sound so sure."

"Basketball hasn't been very much fun." Ashley feels the leather of the ball against her palm. "It has to be different this time."

"So make it different."

"Easy for you to say."

"Well, yeah," says Scotty with a wink. "I'm the queen of different."

★★★

When Ashley gets home, she finds Matt sitting on the couch again.

He looks up at her. "I talked to Mom about the tournament and some of our ideas to cut costs."

"Okay?"

"She said she can contribute seventy-five dollars."

"With the twenty-five I was saving for new basketball shoes, that will cover the tournament fee. But what about the rest of it? And the tournament is two weeks away. I can't save that quickly."

"I'm going to help."

"You don't have to do that."

"Yes, I do," says Matt. He hesitates. "You've been doing my chores."

"You noticed?" asked Ashley. She's not sure whether to feel angry that he's been letting her do them or glad that he noticed the work.

"Yeah," says Matt. His tone suggests he doesn't know whether Ashley will be angry or not either.

There's a silence. Ashley remembers Scotty's wide eyes in the washroom before practice. When Ashley looks at her schedule like an outsider, she sees how crammed it has been. How exhausted she's been. Matt's chores have been one of the things that have made Ashley's schedule so hard to handle.

It has to be different.

"I, um, don't, uh, think, I candoyourchoresany-more," she blurts out.

"What?"

"I — don't think I can do your chores anymore."

Matt slumps his shoulders. "You shouldn't have had to do them up to now in the first place."

Ashley remembers what Scotty said. "Maybe you should talk to mom about it?"

Matt bites his lip. "No. I can do them." He pauses. "Was Stephanie at practice today?"

"Why do you ask?"

"She won't answer my texts."

"Oh," says Ashley. "I guess she's still mad at you, then?"

"I was a real jerk."

"Just tell her you're sorry."

"It's not that easy," says Matt dismissively.

"Maybe not," Ashley shrugs. "But, if you really care about her —"

"I do." A blush fills his cheeks.

"Then I don't think you should give up."

Ashley limps out of the living room, but her thoughts are racing through her mind. Will Matt come through with the money? Will she be able to go to Victoria with the team? Will any of it matter if Ashley can't stay calm on the court?

16 DOING THINGS DIFFERENTLY

Ashley stands outside her math classroom. Her ankle is almost fully healed, and she has been cleared to attend basketball practice the next day. Without the newspaper route or basketball practices, Ashley's muscles feel fresh, like she could go for a long run and still have lots of energy afterwards.

If Mrs. Greene needs me to babysit the normal times, I'll have another fifteen dollars by the end of the week. Not even close to enough.

"Ashley!" squeals a voice from down the hall, breaking Ashley from her thoughts.

Ashley turns. It's the twins. Tanya runs up and wraps Ashley in a hug so big that Ashley stumbles back a few steps.

"Where've you been?" Ashley asks.

"Sick," says Tanya. "Sorry we didn't call! Dad says we can't have our phones when we're home from school."

"How are you feeling?"

"Way better. Dad made us go to the doctor this

morning to be extra sure, and the doctor said we were fine."

"That's awesome."

"Being home from school gets really boring after a day or two," adds Tamara. "I'm so excited to see you."

"You're not mad?"

"Why would we be mad?"

"The last time I saw you, I snapped at you, and I haven't been able to hang out with you. I was so busy, and I'm just really sorry."

"It's okay!" Tanya chirps. Ashley should've known that the twins wouldn't hold a grudge over something as small as being snapped at. "We missed you because you weren't around as much."

"But we get it," adds Tamara.

The twins rarely talk as "we," but Ashley thinks it's cute when they do.

"What are you doing after school today?"

"I'm supposed to shoot around with Scotty, but maybe I could hang out after? We could watch the countdown."

Ashley realizes that after shooting around with Scotty, she's supposed to study. If she hangs out with Tanya and Tamara, she won't have time to do her homework. "No, wait, I can't."

"Oh."

"It's just . . . Why don't you join us?"

"Sounds fun!"

After school, Ashley, Tamara, and Tanya get on the bus to meet Scotty at the outdoor basketball court in her neighbourhood. They chat and laugh the whole bus ride. When they get off the bus, Scotty is waiting for them. As usual, her makeup is bright and multi-coloured.

"Is that her?" whispers Tanya.

Ashley nods. Before Ashley can stop her, Tanya pulls Scotty into a giant hug. Scotty stands completely still with her arms down at her side.

"Whoa, there," says Tamara to her sister. "Give the girl some room to breathe."

Tanya lets go of Scotty, who looks somewhat stunned. "I'm Tanya! Do you really have melt-proof makeup?"

"I do," says Scotty tentatively.

"Where did you get it? Does it feel different when you put it on? Can you mix it with foundation? You have to tell me everything."

Scotty smiles as Ashley and Tamara follow her and Tanya to the basketball court. An unusual tickle of nerves fill Ashley's belly.

What will it feel like to play again? What if it's not fun?

Tanya and Scotty talk non-stop about makeup.

Ashley begins by taking short range shots. Tanya rebounds for Scotty while she practices left-handed layups.

As Scotty misses her seventh layup in a row, she growls in frustration. "This sucks."

"At least you're hitting the rim!" encourages Tanya. Scotty huffs, but tries again. It's hard to give up in the face of Tanya's endless positivity. Tanya turns to Ashley. "How are things going with that bully girl?"

"Jane?" asks Scotty.

"Jane," confirms Ashley.

"Ashley stood up for me last game," says Scotty.

"No way," says Tanya. Scotty retells the story, and Tamara and Tanya listen intently. Ashley focuses on listening and shooting. She feels less nervous with each shot. When Scotty's done, Tanya shrugs. "It's good you called her out."

"I dunno," says Ashley. "There was probably a better way to do it." She thinks about the game against Fraser Valley and Number 7. "I just got mad and did it. Same thing has been happening on the court. If I'm going to stay in the game, I've got to be calm."

"Well, what gets you mad?"

"Jane, mostly." Ashley looks around at Tanya, Tamara, and Scotty. Their heads are tilted to the side, and their expressions are open, ready to listen. Maybe they'll see things differently. "She calls me 'Sneakers.'"

"Why?"

"Because of my shoes. She thinks they're ugly," says Ashley sheepishly.

"The ones you wear in school season?"

"Yeah."

"But, those are the best. You've had them forever."

says Tanya. "I bet they fit perfectly!"

"That's something I would say," says Scotty. "But with a lot less enthusiasm."

"I guess," says Ashley.

"I bet she's only saying it because she's jealous," adds Tanya.

"Of my shoes?" asks Ashley.

"I don't know." Tanya shrugs. "Why else would she do it?"

Ashley remembers Jane getting mad about Maude's shoes. Then she remembers Jane trash-talking Scotty and Ashley in the second tryout. "Maybe she's scared of not being the best? Which is stupid. She's way better than me."

"Not on defence," Scotty points out.

Ashley blushes. "I guess not."

"Yeah," agrees Tamara. "And you were the fastest player on our school team."

"And if you're going to keep stopping people on defence, and beating people to the ball, they're going to get mad at you," adds Tanya.

"How do I stop getting mad back?"

Tamara catches one of Ashley's rebounds and holds on to the ball. She looks at Ashley.

"What?" demands Ashley.

"Well, um, sometimes, you get, uh, a little grumpy when you're tired," says Tamara quickly. "So, maybe you could make sure you're not tired?"

"That would probably help," says Ashley. Tamara grins.

"Remember our last practice," Scotty reminds her.

With a clear mind, Ashley remembers the first time Jane called her "Sneakers."

It was after I stopped her in the Chase drill.

She remembers defending Fraser Valley Number 7.

She got mad because she couldn't score . . . because my defence stopped her from scoring.

Scotty has stopped shooting and stands between Tanya and Tamara. All three girls are totally focused on helping Ashley. Warmth fills Ashley's chest.

"Why are you smiling?" asks Scotty.

"You three are the best."

"True," says Scotty. Tanya and Tamara laugh. "Wanna end with a game of Horse? All four of us can play."

"What's Horse?" asks Tanya.

"It's a shooting game. I'll explain it," replies Scotty. She passes Ashley the ball. The leathery texture feels perfect against her palm.

17 TEARS AND POPCORN

The weekend before the Provincial Tournament, Scotty and Ashley play one-on-one at the outdoor court by Scotty's house. Tanya and Tamara watch from the sidelines.

On defence, Ashley feels alert and rested. Scotty shot-fakes, but Ashley doesn't buy the fake and stays on her feet. Scotty takes a tentative dribble with her left hand and Ashley swats the ball away and runs after it to grab it.

"Ugh!" says Scotty. "That's what I get for using my left hand. But you're so hard to get past."

Even though she feels bad Scotty's fumbled the ball, Ashley also feels a surge of pride.

"That's good," says Tanya encouragingly. "Practice will make you better."

"I just lost the ball."

"But you're winning 6–2, so it's okay if you lose the ball."

"Thanks for pointing that out, Tan," Ashley laughs.

"No problem!" Tanya turns to Scotty. "You're doing

great! Your left hand is going to be so awesome in the tournament."

"So you keep telling me," mumbles Scotty.

The twins laugh, but Ashley's shoulders are tense.

I'm going to carpool with Scotty to the ferry dock, and bring a cooler with food. I won't buy any tournament T-shirts. But, I still don't have enough money for the hotel and travel costs. And I'll need to take some money for meals.

"All right, time to go," says Tanya assertively. "The countdown will be on soon. We have to go."

Maybe I should ask Mrs. Greene if she needs me to baby-sit more . . . No. If I babysit any more, I'll be too busy. Besides, Matt promised he'd help . . . but can I trust him?

"Ash?"

"What?"

"Wade," Tanya says matter-of-factly. "Come on."

"Right," replies Ashley, jogging off the court to join her friends.

***

At the last practice before the Provincial Tournament, the team gathers at centre court to cheer. Even though practice is over, Ashley can't stay still. She fidgets while Coach Catherine talks.

"No matter what happens on the scoreboard this weekend, I want you to go out there, work hard, and have fun! Vancouver on three. One. Two. Three."

"Vancouver!"

"Ashley, can I talk to you for a second?" asks Stephanie.

Ashley nods and joins Stephanie in the corner of the gymnasium. Stephanie takes a deep breath. "The tournament fees are due tomorrow."

"I know," says Ashley. The knot in her stomach tightens. "You can't ask to push the deadline back again, can you?"

"The Provincial Tournament requires the money up front."

"Okay," sighs Ashley. "But I have until tomorrow, right?"

"You do."

"I'll get you the money," says Ashley.

"It's not me." Stephanie smiles gently. "It's the tournament. And, Ash, if you need anything, you can always ask."

"I know. Thanks," says Ashley. Stephanie begins to walk away. "Actually, have you seen Matt this week?"

Stephanie stops instantly. "Not exactly."

"Not exactly?"

"I haven't seen him, but he's been leaving notes in my locker."

"Are you still mad at him?"

"Yes." Stephanie hesitates. "Kind of. I don't know . . ." Stephanie opens her mouth to say something, but then shakes her head. "Aaaaanyways . . . Why do you ask?"

"He was supposed to help me."

"Oh." Stephanie's eyebrows furrow together in worry, but she doesn't say anything else. Ashley's heart sinks. If Stephanie doesn't trust Matt, Ashley shouldn't either. "Well I hope he does."

"Me too."

"Want a ride home?"

Ashley nods. She wants to go home and look at her savings one last time. Maybe she miscounted. Maybe a magic basketball elf left the money for her.

When Ashley gets to the apartment, she walks directly to her room and shuts the door. She picks up the envelope on top of her dresser and pours the money on to her bed.

"Five. Seven. Eleven . . ." Ashley counts each bill and coin. "Fifty-seven dollars and seventy-five cents."

Plus seventy-five from Mom. That's only a hundred and twenty-seven . . . I can't go to Victoria.

Ashley bounces her knee up and down and counts again. "Fifty-seven dollars and seventy-five cents."

Tears well in her eyes.

I should call Tanya and Tamara. But what will they do? I can't ask for their allowance money.

The tears pour down Ashley's cheeks. But, as Ashley sniffles, she smells something strange. Something . . . salty. Ashley gets up and opens her door. The smell gets stronger. Ashley follows the smell to the kitchen.

"Mom?"

"Mom's not home," says Matt, popping his head out of the kitchen. "It's just me."

"Is there popcorn?"

"No."

"Then why does the whole apartment smell like a popcorn factory?"

"None of your business," Matt winks. Then, as though he has just remembered something, his expression becomes very serious. "We need to talk. I think you should sit down."

Ashley walks to her spot on the recliner in the living room. Matt follows and plops down on the couch.

"Is this about the tournament?"

"It is," says Matt.

Ashley uses her sleeve to wipe the tears from her eyes. "I can't go."

"No, you can," says Matt. He adds, "I've been doing your paper route."

"What?"

"I called Mr. Penumbra. I knew he had an opening because one of his workers got hurt," says Matt with a twinkle in his eye. "I asked if I could take her slot. It means getting up a little early —"

"Tell me about it."

"But, I think it's been good to get me out of bed. I got paid today. Between the paper route and my job, it's enough to make up the rest of the two-hundred-dollar fee." Matt pulls an envelope with money out of his bag and holds it in his hand.

For a moment, Ashley is overjoyed, but then she's hit by another emotion: guilt. "I can't take your money."

"You were doing my chores for weeks. How long did it take you each time?"

"I don't know."

"Guess. How much per week would you say?"

"Like, an hour."

"Right. So, really, this is just me paying you back for doing my chores."

"Well, I don't need all of it. With Mom's money, I've got one hundred and twenty-seven dollars and seventy-five cents."

"So, you only need seventy-five bucks. What a deal!" He takes out the money and hands Ashley one hundred and twenty-five dollars.

"This is more than I need for the fee."

"You'll need to eat more than what you're taking in that cooler. And buy yourself one of those stupid tournament T-shirts," says Matt, smiling. "So, I was wondering . . ." Matt clears his throat. "Once you're done basketball, maybe you could start doing my chores again?"

Ashley doesn't really want to do Matt's chores, but he did just pay her tournament fee. Besides, once basketball is over, her schedule won't be as busy. "Okay, I guess."

"Just for a little bit," adds Matt quickly. "Just long enough for me to go to morning physiotherapy. I might not get a big university scholarship, but I could get healthy enough to play soccer again. I really miss playing."

Ashley's face brightens into a smile. "I miss watching you play."

Matt puts the envelope on the table. He pulls a second, much larger envelope out of his bag. "And, I need you to give this to Stephanie for me."

"What is it?"

"You'll see."

Ashley tries to hide her excitement, but her voice comes out as a squeal. "Okay!"

She's going to Victoria!

18 THE CHAMPIONSHIP TOURNAMENT

Ashley stands at centre court waiting for the ball in warmup. Above her, there is a jumbotron screen where highlights from the game are played. The stadium-style seating is filled with other teams and coaches, causing the whole gym to buzz. It is impossibly more exciting than her dream.

"Ashley!" yells Coach Catherine from the bench. Immediately, Ashley jogs to her. "I want you to be ready to guard Number 10."

Ashley watches the Burnaby team warm up and looks for Number 10. When a girl with broad shoulders scores a powerful layup, Ashley looks at Coach Catherine. "You want me to guard Kelly?"

"I do. You won't be starting the game, so I want you to take the first couple minutes to watch her play."

"Okay."

The horn buzzes and the Vancouver team jogs to the bench.

Coach Catherine clears her throat and the team

quiets to listen. "I can't think of a better way to start the Provincial Tournament than to get a rematch against Burnaby. They're a good team with strong players." Coach Catherine looks directly at Ashley. "But we're a good team too, and we've improved since we played them last. Work hard. Work smart. Work together. If we do those three things, I believe we can win this game."

The starters line up on the court and Ashley takes her seat beside Maude. On the court, Jane is extra loud. She marches up to the centre circle to line up across from Kelly and looks her straight in the eye. Jane's expression is tight: her eyes are narrow and her mouth is clamped shut. Unlike Jane, Kelly's expression is focused but relaxed.

The referee walks to the centre circle and tosses the ball into the air. Jane and Kelly jump. Kelly gets her hand on the ball first and tips it forward to a teammate. She immediately charges down the court. Caught on her heels, Jane is behind. The Burnaby team makes three passes before the ball winds up back in Kelly's hands underneath the basket. She scores.

"She's good," says Maude to no one in particular.

"She really is," replies Ashley.

On the court, Scotty gets the ball. The Burnaby defender immediately jumps to Scotty's right side. Scotty looks at the open left side but chooses to go right. The Burnaby defender steals the ball and drives to the basket. She scores a layup. 4–0 for Burnaby.

Scotty gets the ball and immediately passes it up court to Jane. Jane takes two dribbles. When her toe touches the three-point line, she shoots. The quick shot is off-balance and it clanks off the rim before the Vancouver players can get in position to rebound. Kelly runs toward the basket and grabs the rebound, sprinting up court for a layup.

"Timeout!" yells Coach Catherine. The referee blows her whistle to stop the game. The players jog to their benches. Coach Catherine looks down the bench. "Ashley, sub in for Paige."

Ashley nods and jogs to the scorer's bench. Before she can return to the huddle, Stephanie joins her. "Kelly is a good player. You can't expect to stop her completely. Just limit her shots."

The horn buzzes to signal the end of the timeout.

Ashley walks onto the court. Just like in warmup, she feels the buzz of the excitement that fills the gym. She takes the ball out of bounds and passes it to Scotty. Again, Scotty's defender forces her left. Scotty takes one dribble right and her defender immediately swats it out of bounds. The ball bounces away from the court and the referee is forced to chase after it.

"Come on, Scotty," says Jane harshly.

Anger bubbles in Ashley's throat. Ashley notices the feeling and swallows it. She jogs to Scotty. "I'm going to pass you the ball. Pass it right back. I can bring it up the court."

"You're not the point guard," argues Scotty.

"I can still dribble," points out Ashley. "I'll get it over half-court. Then I'll pass it back to you."

Scotty sprints to get open. Ashley passes her the ball and steps inbounds. Scotty gladly passes it back to Ashley. Ashley isn't used to dribbling the ball under pressure, but she manages to get it up court.

"1-4!" yells Ashley.

Ashley passes the ball to Scotty. Scotty stands for a moment at the top of the three-point line. She stares at the basket. Her defender is standing so far on the right side of Scotty's body that she's practically inviting Scotty to take the ball to the left side of the rim.

Scotty takes a tentative dribble to her left. Though she lacks power and confidence, her defender is cheating so far to the right, it doesn't matter. Scotty drives to the basket. Ashley sees that Tanya was right. After all her practice, Scotty's layups have gotten better. The ball hits the back board, clanks off the rim, and falls through the mesh of the hoop.

6–2 for Vancouver.

"Good job," yells Ashley over her shoulder as she runs back on defence. She immediately finds Kelly and sticks to her like glue. Everywhere Kelly goes, Ashley is right there. Another Burnaby player is forced to take an off-balance shot.

The pace of the game is fast and intense, but Ashley's muscles feel ready. When she's subbed back into the game in the fourth quarter, the score is 40–38 for Vancouver.

Jane receives the ball on the wing. Kelly guards her tightly. Jane drives at the basket, but Kelly stays with her. Jane jumps to shoot, and Kelly jumps at the same moment. She blocks Jane's shot and the ball bounces toward the sideline. Before it can go out of bounds, Kelly runs after the ball. She picks it up and dribbles down the court. Ashley sprints after her. Kelly is two steps ahead of Ashley, and Ashley knows she won't be able to catch Kelly. As Kelly jumps into the air, Ashley jumps to challenge the shot, but she's careful not to foul her.

Kelly scores. With forty-five seconds left in the game, the game is tied.

"Timeout!" yells the Burnaby coach.

As Ashley turns to jog to the Vancouver bench, Jane confronts her. "Come on, Sneakers. If you can't stop her, take your ugly kicks and get out of the game."

Ashley opens her mouth to yell at Jane. In the corner of her eye, she sees Scotty jogging toward them. She remembers what Tamara and Tanya said. Jane's just mad because she doesn't want Kelly to be better than her and she's taking it out on Ashley. Ashley looks Jane square in the eyes.

She takes a breath. "I don't like being called Sneakers, and I'm doing my best. Just like you."

Jane's mouth hangs open like a guppy fish.

"Come on, Jane and Ashley!" yells Coach Catherine.

Jane and Ashley jog to the bench. "We've got the ball. I want to run 1-4. Scotty, do your best to beat your defender. Everyone else, get ready to shoot!"

The horn sounds and the players return to the court. Scotty looks nervous. Ashley can only imagine the pressure Scotty feels as the point guard.

Ashley jogs over and holds out her and to Scotty for a high-five. "You got this."

"I better," mumbles Scotty.

The referee hands Paige the ball out of bounds. She passes to Scotty. Everyone else jogs to their positions. Scotty looks to the right; her defender is there. Scotty hesitates, but then bounces the ball with her left hand. In two determined — if slightly awkward — dribbles, she's underneath the basket. Kelly is running toward her to block the shot, but Scotty goes up with her left hand, protecting the ball with her right hand.

She scores! Vancouver leads 42–40.

With ten seconds left in the game, Burnaby sprints up the court. Ashley finds Kelly and stays as close to her as possible. Kelly receives the ball on the wing. Ashley can't look up at the clock, but she knows time is running out. Kelly looks at the rim, but doesn't dribble. There's a commotion behind Ashley, but her mind is clear. She stays focused on the ball. Suddenly, Kelly passes the ball away.

Ashley turns her head. Behind her, Jane's check is wide open under the rim. She catches the ball and shoots. Jane jumps to block the shot, and the Burnaby player is spooked. Ashley watches the ball clank against the rim. There's going to be a rebound. Kelly moves to chase the ball. Ashley goes with her. Kelly uses her size to try and get position, but Ashley's legs feel strong. She uses her speed to manoeuvre in front of Kelly. Everything is clear. She just needs to focus. As the ball hits the rim, Ashley and Kelly both jump. Kelly reaches to grab the ball, but Ashley puts up her hands and tips the ball away.

The score clock sounds. Vancouver has won the game!

After shaking hands with the Burnaby team, the players gather around Coach Catherine. "You should be really proud not of the score, but of how we played! Now, let's go get dinner."

Energy bursts through Ashley's body. If this is how it feels to win the first game of the championship tournament, she can't imagine how it would feel to win the final. She hopes she'll get to find out.

At the restaurant, Ashley sits beside Scotty. The rest of the girls order big main courses, but on the way to the restaurant, Ashley ate a granola bar and a banana. She orders an appetizer.

"That last rebound was awesome," says Scotty.

"So was your layup."

"It was so awkward."

Suddenly, Ashley's phone buzzes in her pocket. It's

a text message from Matt. Ashley begins to type her response.

"No phones at team dinner," chides Stephanie.

"But, it's Matt. He's asking about the game."

"Answer after we're done."

Ashley puts away her phone. "Actually, he wanted me to give you something." Ashley rummages through her backpack and takes out the envelope.

"What's this?"

"He wouldn't tell me."

Stephanie slowly opens the envelope. As soon as she looks inside, her eyes open wide.

"What is it?"

Stephanie pulls a photograph out of the envelope and shows it to Ashley. In the photo, Matt stands behind the kitchen table. In front of him, "I'm sorry" is spelled out in popcorn. In the envelope, there is also a letter and a small bag of popcorn.

Stephanie reads the letter. She blushes, the same way she did when the handsome boy in the stands was waiting for her.

"What's the letter say?"

"It's between me and Matt . . . for now."

"He asked you out, didn't he?!" asks Ashley excitedly.

"Shhhh," hushes Stephanie, but she's so red that Ashley is sure the answer is yes.

At the other end of the table, Jane chats with a group of girls. "Did you see me get that rebound in the third quarter?! It was the turning point." The girls' eyes are glued to Jane, nodding and smiling along with every word.

Scotty gently elbows Ashley in the ribs. "Wish you were sitting down there?"

"Not even a little."

"So," begins Stephanie, "how does it feel to play in your first provincial tournament?"

"Solid," replies Scotty. "The whole season's been really good."

"Yeah . . ." begins Ashley, but she hesitates. She thinks about the look on her mom's face when she read the team participation fee, getting up early for the newspaper route, the practices after babysitting where her whole body felt like an anchor, and being teased about her basketball shoes. "Well, parts of the season weren't so . . . solid."

Then, Ashley remembers laughing and shooting around with Tanya, Tamara, and Scotty, and working with Matt to help cut the cost of the tournament fee.

She thinks about Jane.

I didn't let her get to me this time.

A surge of pride pulses through Ashley's body. Ashley smiles as she thinks about getting the rebound at the end of the game and being on the court with her teammates.

"But it's been really good too. I think even the ugly stuff was worth every minute."

CHECK OUT THESE OTHER GIRLS BASKETBALL STORIES FROM LORIMER'S SPORTS STORIES SERIES:

Fadeaway
by Steven Barwin

Renna's the captain of her basketball team, and is known to run a tight ship. But then a new girl from a rival team joins. Suddenly, Renna's being left out and picked on by her own teammates. Can she face this bullying and win her team back before it goes too far?

Home Court Advantage
by Sandra Diersch

Life as a foster child can be tough — so Debbie has learned to be tough back, both at home and on the court. But when a nice couple decides to adopt her, Debbie suddenly isn't so sure of herself — and her new teammates aren't so sure about her either.

Jump Ball
by Adrienne Mercer

Basketball is more than just a game for Abby, it's everything. When her younger sister makes it onto the school basketball team, Abby can't help fighting to be the best — even if it means fighting against her own teammates.

Pick and Roll
by Kelsey Blair

Jazz Smith-Mohapatra is the toughest and best player on her basketball team — and this year she's determined to lead the team to a championship win. But in the last game of the regular season, she sets a pick and roll that seriously hurts her opponent. Now Jazz is facing a Fair Play Commission hearing and possible suspension. Even worse, her teammates are suddenly questioning her physical style of play and their chances of winning the championship.

Queen of the Court
by Michele Martin Bossley

Kallana's father has suddenly decided that joining the basketball team will be a "character-building" experience for her. But she can't dribble, she can't sink a basket, and worst of all, she will have to wear one of those hideous uniforms…

Rebound
by Adrienne Mercer

C.J.'s just been made captain of the basketball team — but her teammate, Debi, seems determined to make C.J. miserable. Then C.J. wakes up one morning barely able to stand up. How can she show Debi up when she can't even make it onto the court?

Slam Dunk
by Steven Barwin & Gabriel David Tick

The Raptors are going co-ed — which means that for the first time ever, there will be *girls* on the team. Mason's willing to see what these girls can do, but the other guys on the team aren't so sure about this…